Rosie's Gift

About the Author

Ann Carroll is married with two children and lives in Dublin where she teaches English in Killinarden Community School. This is her third *Rosie* book published by Poolbeg.

Rosie's Gift

Ann Carroll

POOLBEG

Published 1997 by
Poolbeg Press Ltd
123 Baldoyle Industrial Estate
Dublin 13, Ireland

The Publishers gratefully acknowledge the support of The Arts Council.

A catalogue record for this book is available from the British Library.

ISBN 1 85371 875 0

Cover illustration by David Axtell
Cover design by Poolbeg Group Services Ltd
Set by Poolbeg Group Services Ltd in Goudy 10.5/13
Printed by The Guernsey Press Ltd,
Vale, Guernsey, Channel Islands.

For all the staff and students at
Killinarden Community School,
in appreciation of their support
and encouragement

Cast of Characters

Rosie McGrath: Heroine of *Rosie's Quest* and *Rosie's Troubles*.
Mom and Dad.
Gran.
Mr Murray: Rosie's teacher and tutor at Collins' Community School.
Ms O'Grady: The young science teacher.
David Byrne: A boy in Rosie's class. She has mixed feelings about him.
The Warden, at Oak Park hostel, where Rosie and her class go on Outdoor Ed.
Joseph O'Neill: Rosie's ancestor who worked as a gardener's boy in Oak Park in 1870, when it was a big estate.
Jane O'Neill: Joseph's sister, a maid in Oak Park.
Lady de Courcy: Owner of Oak Park in 1870.
Cyril de Courcy: Her son, a mean malicious young man, who hates Joseph O'Neill and wants to destroy him.
Florence de Courcy: The eleven-year-old daughter of Lady de Courcy.
Miss Payne: Florence's governess, who conspires with Cyril to ruin Joseph and his sister.
Mr Harvey, *Mrs Biddle*, *Mrs Smiley:* Servants at Oak Park.

Chapter 1

"OUTDOOR ED for a whole week. Sound!"

"Ah sir, that's great! No classes."

"No homework. Deadly!"

"On our own. No adults. Brilliant!"

Mr Murray, class 1E's tutor and PE teacher, frowned. "*I* am an adult," he said, "as is Ms O'Grady, your Science teacher, and we shall be there with you all the time, keeping a very severe eye on things."

Mr Murray couldn't be severe if he tried, Rosie thought. He looked too young. Maybe he'd been a child genius and gone to college at fourteen.

"But it won't be like having a real adult in charge," said David Byrne, who had no tact. "I mean, you're not narky, sir. Not like Mr King and Ms Proby. And you can do somersaults. I bet they can't."

The class sniggered. Mr King and Ms Proby were very strict and middle aged. They moved sedately, expecting all pupils to step promptly out of their way and stand to attention. Woe betide any who didn't. Certainly, they were not given to doing somersaults.

"It's part of my job to teach acrobatics," Mr Murray said, "and it's also part of my job to get you lot fit. Every day we shall be climbing the Wicklow mountains hail, rain or snow –"

"Snow? In the last week of October, Sir?"

"Jogging through forests," Mr Murray ignored the interruption. "Wading through streams and rivers, orienteering, hiking, grappling with the elements. At the end you will be as fit as Tarzan!"

"Will we be swinging from trees on ropes? I always wanted to do that." David Byrne's excitement was growing.

"You will not. But you will be doing something equally exciting, something you have probably never attempted before David, and which is therefore very dangerous."

The boy was beside himself with excitement. "What Sir? What?"

Sir looked solemn,"You will be cooking your own dinner every evening."

Rosie groaned. If she had to do her own cooking she'd be poisoned early on. David Byrne was just as depressed. "I bet Tarzan never cooked. I bet Jane did it for him." He brightened, "The girls could do ours, Sir."

The girls booed, while the boys grinned.

Mr Murray raised a hand, "What a good idea. They will boil the potatoes for all of us every evening and the boys will peel them. How about that?"

This time there was a cheer from the girls and filthy looks from the boys directed at David, who muttered, "I was only messing, Sir."

"Can Ms O'Grady climb and wade and grapple with things?" Rosie asked.

Ms O'Grady was slim and young and, in Rosie's opinion, looked more like a ballet dancer than Tarzan.

"Ms O'Grady is super fit!" Mr Murray stated, his eyes lighting up. "She could run up those mountains if she wanted. She'll fly over all obstacles – "

"You fancy Miss, don't you, Sir?" David Byrne honestly wanted to know.

Mr Murray went bright scarlet. He opened his mouth to say something, but couldn't find the words.

He really does fancy her, Rosie thought. Then, feeling

sorry for his embarrassment, she said, "Tell us about the hostel, Sir. What's it like?"

Recovering quickly, Mr Murray smiled sweetly at his class, "Haunted."

He said nothing more and his eyes took on a faraway look, as if he were seeing beyond them.

"Haunted!" David Byrne gasped. "You mean ghosts?"

"Well I don't mean chickens!" Mr Murray was scornful. Then he lowered his voice so they had to strain to hear.

"Oak Park was once a fine old house, part of a huge estate. But towards the end of the last century, the owner drank and gambled his way through a fortune. He was a cruel man and thought the way to survive was to work his servants to the bone. Until the awful night one of them waited for him in the shadow of the great staircase . . ."

He paused for effect.

"Sir!"

"What happened, Sir?"

"Tell us, Sir! Don't be so mean."

"Well, Cyril de Courcy – that was the owner's name – stopped for a moment at the top of the stairs to steady himself. He was very drunk. The moonlight shone through the long landing window. De Courcy studied his reflection in the glass, no doubt thinking what a fine man he was. Then he saw another face, one twisted with hatred. Out of the shadows stepped his murderer and with one mighty effort he pushed de Courcy down the marble stairs. His head bounced off every step and when he came to rest at the bottom, he was quite dead. Even today you can see traces of his blood where it seeped into the marble."

"That is a lovely story," Rosie said, quite fascinated.

"Deadly!" The others agreed.

"Stupid!" David Byrne said. "His head wouldn't bounce. It wasn't a football. It's a sap story!"

Mr Murray turned to him, "So you won't mind sleeping on

your own in the garret room that the murderer is supposed to haunt?"

The boy paled and the teacher felt sorry for him. "Don't worry. I shall probably take that room myself. Of course there are many stories about the way Cyril de Courcy died. Who knows which of them is true?"

Then he added very softly, "On our first night in Oak Park, after we've eaten supper and we're gathered around the fire and the shadows are playing on the walls I shall tell you another story, much more frightening than this. A story about a young boy, not much older than you, who was treated so unfairly by the same Cyril de Courcy, that his ghost still returns to look for . . . JUSTICE!"

He roared the last word at them, so that they all jumped. Gratified at the reaction, he went on, "Now, class 1E. I see this trip as a bonding experience. After all, this is your first term in Collins' Community School and you don't know one another yet, not properly. But after this week away, I can promise you – " he made it sound more like a threat – "we will know each other very well."

A bonding experience? Rosie looked at David Byrne who was now mimicking his tutor, playing for laughs and not getting any. Sometimes he was such a sap, she thought. Nothing would bond her to him, not even superglue.

So far, Rosie loved her new school. After primary, it was wonderful not to see the teachers for more than forty minutes at a time in most subjects. And there were so many things to do after hours, like drama and games. Having Mr Murray as tutor was a bonus. He was deadly. He treated them as special and every Wednesday he ran a gymnastics club just for them. Not only did he show them how to do multiple somersaults, he got them to climb ropes and do acrobatics on the bars. Best of all, he taught them to walk on their hands for five minutes at a time.

Of course, he wasn't at all pleased when he saw David Byrne walking on his hands down the corridor, especially when Mr King stopped to comment acidly, "Ah, you must be Mr Murray's student. I'd recognise one anywhere. It's their method of locomotion. Has a disastrous effect on traffic though. Detention for you at 3.30, my boy. And if you value your freedom, you'll arrive at my room the right way up!"

He swept on, brushing aside Mr Murray who glared at the hapless boy. "Serves you right. Nitwit! I suppose I should be glad you weren't swinging out of the lights. Catching the gleam in David's eye, he added, "Don't even *dream* of it."

Remembering, Rosie smiled. David might be a pain but sometimes he could be good fun.

She liked her class. She liked Mr Murray. Some day she might even like David Byrne.

The Outdoor Ed trip would be great. She couldn't wait to get home and tell Mom, Dad and Gran about it.

"Oak Park in Wicklow," Gran mused. "I thought the place was derelict."

It was later that night. Mom and Dad were out and Rosie and her grandmother were in the sitting-room having supper.

"It's been fixed up as a hostel," Rosie said. "We're the first visitors to use it. Mr Murray told us."

"How odd that you should be going there. My grandmother, Jane O'Neill, was a maid in that house in 1870 and her brother Joseph was the odd-job boy. She was thirteen, the same age as you, and he was two years older." She paused and Rosie waited, knowing how Gran liked to sort out her thoughts when telling a story.

"Their parents were dead. I don't know the details, but anyway Joseph and his sister were alone in the world."

Rosie was more interested in Oak Park. "Was it a nice place to work, Gran?"

"For a while. Then it brought them bad luck. Mind you, I'm only going by what Mother told me. She heard bits and pieces of what happened from Jane, who found a lot of the details too upsetting to share. Mother tried to fill in the gaps, though I'm not sure how accurate she was. But it's a sad story all the same."

Again the old lady stopped and Rosie began to feel impatient.

Gran is like Mr Murray, she thought, stopping just when things get interesting.

"From all accounts," Gran at last continued, "Joseph was a bright strong boy who got on with everyone."

"There was an enormous number of servants on the estate when they started working there: labourers, supervisors, field workers, head gardeners, undergardeners, grooms, carpenters, dairymaids etc. Someone as lowly as the odd-job boy would never in the ordinary course of events have come to Lady de Courcy's notice. But his sister, Jane, became one of young Florence de Courcy's maids. Florence took a shine to her. She was only eleven and there were no children her own age to play with. She began to treat Jane more as a companion than a maid. And of course Jane talked a lot about her big brother – how he'd looked after her when their parents died, and the adventures they'd shared when they left home to find employment.

"Florence insisted on meeting Joseph and found him every bit as interesting as his sister had said. She began spending as much time as possible with the two of them. They became great friends, which made what happened even worse."

Gran stopped, reflecting on the past.

"I thought you said you didn't know any details," Rosie murmured.

"Not about later events. And I never met Grandmother. She died before I was born, but Mother said she was always talking about life in the big house before disaster struck.

"You see, Florence's brother, Cyril de Courcy, who was seventeen at the time, didn't think the brother and sister were suitable friends for Florence. Since his father's death in a hunting accident, Cyril had considered himself lord and master of the estate and behaved like a tyrant whenever his mother wasn't there. He treated servants with contempt and stories of his behaviour are still told."

"Anyway, he thought Joseph and Jane were common and rough. They hadn't been to school and couldn't read or write. Cyril couldn't tolerate the fact that his sister treated them as equals and he complained to his mother."

"Lady de Courcy said she would see to matters and that was how Joseph first came to her attention. Then, before she had time to discourage the friendship, something happened that made her favour the odd-job boy. Apparently Joseph was very brave and quick thinking on two occasions. 'The hero of the hour,' Lady de Courcy called him. I don't know exactly what happened, but everyone praised Joseph. Unfortunately, Cyril had been present both times and had behaved like a coward.

He hated Joseph for showing him up and went on and on about the boy – "a mere servant" – trying to make him look a fool. Lady de Courcy told him to stop his nonsense. She rewarded Joseph and said nothing at all to her daughter about unsuitable friendships."

Gran stopped to rest her voice and Rosie began to wonder. Mr Murray had mentioned Cyril de Courcy and a boy he had badly treated. Was Joseph that boy?

Gathering breath, Gran continued, "From that time on Cyril de Courcy was so jealous he could no longer be civil to the boy. He told anyone who'd listen that Joseph was a bad lot and would bring ill luck to the family.

"This is where the story becomes unreliable. Mother told me Jane would not speak about what happened next. But some years after her death an old lady called to enquire about her. She had worked as a maid in Oak Park when they were both young and apparently Jane had confided in her just before she left.

"Mother gave the old lady tea and she told her about Jane and her brother and the awful events of that October. She rambled a bit and was confused at times, but as far as Mother could see this is what happened.

"Cyril made no secret of wanting to get rid of Joseph. Lady de Courcy had a priceless diamond necklace, given to her by her husband on their first wedding anniversary. One evening it was robbed from her room and Great-uncle Joseph was blamed. There was a witness – Florence's governess. Joseph's room was searched, but nothing was found. Yet what the governess said was damning. The boy protested his innocence, but Cyril called the constabulary and, to avoid arrest, he was forced to flee.

"Some time before he was accused, Joseph had fixed his sister's cedar wood box for her and left it back in her room. It was a heavy box with all sorts of compartments. Florence had given it to her as a birthday present and had painted the initial 'J' on the lid. One of the hinges had broken and she'd asked her brother to mend it.

"Later, heartbroken at the turn of events, Jane opened the cedar wood box, the last reminder of her brother's kindness. Inside, in a velvet pouch, was the diamond necklace. The poor girl was shocked and for a moment she even believed her brother had taken it. After all, this was clear evidence."

"But how could she believe he was the thief?" Rosie burst in. "Her own brother. Was she brain dead? She must've known Cyril de Courcy set him up. Miserable creep!"

Smiling slightly at Rosie's fierce indignation, Gran said, "Of course she did, once she started thinking. She was only brain dead for a little while, out of shock. But there was worse to come.

"Before Jane decided what to do about the necklace, Cyril de Courcy came looking for her. Told her he knew of Joseph's whereabouts and if she didn't leave the house that same day, he'd have Joseph arrested. He could have been lying, because he wouldn't tell her where Joseph was, but then he was mean enough for that and anyway she couldn't take the chance.

"Cyril insisted she leave without saying goodbye to Florence or Lady de Courcy. She waited till dark, but when she went to pack her belongings, the cedarwood box was empty. The necklace was gone. She was devastated. Somehow, she had hoped to put it back where it belonged and clear her brother's name. But no one ever saw it again.

"Jane went to Dublin and every so often stories drifted back to Oak Park.

"One of the servants had met her on the streets and she was homeless. She had no reference and had to survive by begging. Then someone else heard a kind Quaker lady rescued her and found her a place to eat and sleep and used her influence to get Jane a job as a domestic servant. Where, no one knew.

"But the maid never forgot her and in later years tracked down her address through the Society of Friends – the Quakers.

"That was as much as she could tell Mother. But so much of what she said was hearsay and rumour that Mother didn't know what was true and what wasn't.

"Oh, Jane had told her she'd gone to Dublin and eventually found a job, but she hadn't given any details. She had worked as a servant till she married. And I don't think she ever saw her brother again."

Gran sighed at the sadness of it all. Questions crowded Rosie's mind. What happened to Joseph? And what became of Florence? Why did the necklace never turn up? And was Cyril de Courcy really murdered? Was Joseph the boy who still haunted Oak Park?

In her eagerness to find out, she gabbled at Gran, who did her best to provide the answers.

"I think Joseph joined the British army and was posted abroad. Jane said he'd always wanted to be a soldier."

"I've become as curious as you are, Rosie, to know what happened to him. I've even gone to the Gilbert Library a few times to look up old newspapers, just in case there's a reference there. But so far, I've had no luck.

"From what she heard, Mother thought Cyril de Courcy may have taken the necklace from Jane's box. Perhaps he sold it abroad, somewhere it wouldn't be traced. If he did, the money did him no good.

"He was killed all right, but it was an accident. When he was drunk one evening he fell down the marble staircase and cracked his head. He was so hated, it pleased people to think he might have been murdered. But the coroner recorded a verdict of accidental death, according to the newspapers. As to ghosts, I never heard of any at Oak Park. Perhaps your teacher is making it up so that your visit is more exciting.

"Regarding Florence, the old lady told Mother that Florence had gone to live in London with relatives and the estate had been sold to pay Cyril's debts. What happened to the necklace remains a mystery, I'm afraid."

"But that's a tragic story," Rosie said.

"Yes. As far as we know, Joseph's name was never cleared. Perhaps you'd like to see a drawing Jane did of him? She passed it on to Mother who gave it to me."

When Rosie nodded, Gran left the room, returning shortly with a smallish sheet of thick paper.

"It's only his face, but it's quite good and will give you some idea of what Joseph looked like."

Rosie studied the drawing. The boy was smiling, but a small frown creased his forehead as if he found life to be a sometimes serious matter. His eyes had a dreamy quality, his hair was thick and unruly. There was nothing mean or hidden in his expression. She trusted the open smiling features. She'd like to have known Joseph.

The old lady saw her interest. "Keep the picture if you like, Rosie."

"Why did you never tell me all this before, Gran?"

"Because it's a painful subject. One way or another that necklace caused such tragedy. Joseph was hunted as a thief and Jane lost her closest relative, her job and her friend, Florence. I knew we had to talk about it some day and your trip to Oak Park gave me the opportunity. I wouldn't like you to have gone there without knowing what the place meant to our family."

For a while there was silence, both of them brooding on the past. Gazing at Rosie's sombre face, Gran sought to lighten her mood a little.

"That drawing is your only inheritance from Joseph," she smiled, "unless you count the gift he was supposed to have. Not that I ever believed in it."

"What gift?" Rosie was barely listening, still pondering the mystery of the missing necklace.

"Oh, apparently he could travel to the past, even to the future. Daft! I think maybe he'd heard of Jules Verne and wanted to impress his young sister . . . what's the matter, Rosie?"

Rosie was finding it difficult to swallow. Her face went a deep red, then paled and her eyes grew enormous.

"What is it, child?" Gran became agitated. "Are you not feeling well? It's my fault blathering on about the family. I should have noticed the time and you should have been asleep long ago. Up to bed at once with you!"

Rosie gripped the arms of her chair, refusing to move, still unable to speak.

"Don't open and close your mouth like a fish, child. What is it?"

Her granddaughter gurgled. Gran leaped out of her chair and whacked her on the back. Rosie cried out in pain.

"That's better. Something must have gone against your breath. A cup of tea will soothe you and then you must go to bed."

While Gran was out of the room, Rosie tried to digest the news she'd been given so casually, as an afterthought to Gran's main story. Her great-great-uncle Joseph could travel through time! If this were true then, as Gran said, it was her inheritance. It was a family gift and not some strange magic Rosie had found all on her own.

As soon as she came back with the tea, anxious that her

grandchild should not think she was a foolish gullible old woman, Gran said, "Of course, that time-travelling business is crazy. I never believed any of it. Jane didn't either. She told Mother what Joseph told her – that the gift was supposed to pass down through the family, though sometimes it could skip generations."

Rosie nodded, as if agreeing with Gran that it was all absurd. Inside, excitement welled.

Soon she would be going on the class trip to Oak Park. If she could make another journey to the past while she was there, then she could meet Joseph, talk to him about their mutual gift. He would know exactly what it was like. He would understand the excitement and the fear.

Another idea gripped her. What if she solved the mystery of the necklace? Even better, what if she managed to prevent Cyril ever taking it from his mother's room? Joseph's good name would not be lost. He and his sister could stay together.

The journey back would not be easy. There was a risk that she could lose her way and end up in the wrong century. Twice before she had gone and each time the sense of danger had been acute, like travelling through a pitch black tunnel with no idea of what lay ahead, or jumping off a high cliff with a parachute that might – or might not – open.

But if she was successful, then once again, she could try to change the past . . .

Chapter 2

THE NIGHT before the class trip, Rosie packed her rucksack. She placed the drawing of Joseph in a small notebook, so that it wouldn't crease, and zipped it into the inside pocket of her rucksack. Reckoning the nineteenth century might be short on the kind of food she liked, Rosie stuffed the bag with crisps and chocolate and bubble gum, sour fizz bags, six cans of coke, cheddar and caramel flavoured popcorn and a few packets of chocolate Kimberly biscuits, at this moment her favourite food in all the world.

I wish I could take the toilet, she thought gloomily, I bet there won't be a single toilet in the whole house. In 1920 there had been a very embarrassing episode with Catherine over the chamber pots. *And* they'll have horrible knickers. Rosie groaned. In 1956 she'd found herself in a thick woolly pair with legs halfway down to her knees and elastic so tight it had left ridges. Horrible. And 1920 was the pits! Long baggy poverty stricken bloomers with holes in them. This time, she vowed, I am going to bring plenty of normal knickers!

Rosie had noticed that on each journey she'd made, the clothes she wore had changed, but the things she brought with her did not. Which was why she took as many knickers as she could find in the hot press.

Deciding there would be time too to have a little fun with Mr Murray, Rosie packed the tape recorder Dad had given her for Christmas. So small, it sat snugly in the palm of her hand, yet it was powerful enough to pick up sound over a distance of yards and relay it loudly and clearly. She had wanted it for the Point, so she could tape her favourite group, live. But so far Mom wouldn't let her go, on account of what she called "surf boarding and crowd mashing". Rosie had asked her to at least get the words right and did she know what she was talking about? Mom got very snotty and said she knew cheek when she heard it and Rosie had realised it was time to retreat.

But at least she could record Mr Murray telling one of his stories, or singing a song. He was a truly upsetting singer. Often when class 1E was ready to collapse after a strenuous PE session, Mr Murray would amuse himself by shrieking his version of "Climb Every Mountain" at them. He knew all the words of the "Teddy Bears' Picnic" and insisted on teaching the song to them at tutorial, until the demented teacher in the next classroom banged on the door and begged him to stop the hysterical squealing. Rosie knew now she hadn't much of an ear for music, but she realised Mr Murray's was totally missing when he told her – much to the mirth of the rest of the class – that she had a very sweet voice. Maybe hearing himself on tape would stop the torment.

"Listen carefully 1E. The bus will stop at the forest park. We shall hike from there to the hostel over the two mountains, Maulin and Djouce. Put your picnics into your small haversacks and the driver will take everything else to the hostel. Don't forget to thank him, or he might not come back for us on Saturday."

Mr Murray was standing at the top of the aisle, issuing instructions. He looked like a poster Rosie had once seen advertising Austria. Dressed like a Tyrolean mountaineer, he wore corduroy trousers that fastened just below the knees, long thick woolly socks and heavy boots. He'd also got a tight haircut, probably meant to make him look older, but Rosie thought he resembled a very tall four-year-old.

Of course the minute he'd seen his teacher, David Byrne had started slagging. "Where'd you get the threads, sir? Are you in an opera?" And a second later, "Did you get your hair cut, Sir?" Since the answer was obvious, Mr Murray didn't reply. The boy persisted, till someone else, exasperated, said, "No, he washed it in Persil and it shrank! Now will you shut up about it." But David wouldn't give in. Irritated, the teacher at last gave him the answer he wanted. "Yes, David, I did get my hair cut. Satisfied?" This handed the boy his opening. "Yes sir. But I wouldn't be if I were you, sir. Looks like a lawnmower job!"

Once started, he couldn't be stopped and he turned his attentions to Ms O'Grady. "Miss, are you going out with Sir?" He was unaffected by her cold stare. "He took a real reddener, Miss, when I said he fancied you. He's mad into you Miss. Always looking at you." He was shouting, aware of an attentive audience. Everyone turned to stare at Mr Murray. If it had been night time, his face would've lit up the bus.

The boy was sitting right behind Rosie and Ms O'Grady was standing beside him, ready to lift her bag off the luggage rack. Now she leaned over and spoke so quietly, Rosie had to stretch to hear. "Well, the only one *I'll* be looking at today is you, David Byrne. You make any more of those comments and I'll have you running up and down those mountains like a goat. Do you understand?"

He didn't. With an infallible belief in his own wit, he started again, at increased volume.

"Bet sir got his hair cut just for you, Miss – "

"That's enough!" Mr Murray came storming down. It was the first time Rosie had seen him lose his temper. "There is no way you are going to torment Ms O'Grady for a week, David Byrne. Now you can just stay on this bus and go back home with the driver. He will leave you at the school and explain matters to the principal."

He turned to have a word with the driver.

"Ah, Miss, stop him. I didn't mean it, Miss. Ah, don't let him send me back. I'll be killed. I'm always getting into trouble for being cheeky. I'll be grounded forever. Please Miss. Ask him!"

Ms O'Grady raised a cool eyebrow. "And if I do, what do you promise in return?"

"I'll be perfect. I won't say anything smart. I won't do anything. I won't even breathe. Miss, don't let him send me back."

She went up to Mr Murray. The two teachers and the driver conferred. Rosie felt sorry for David. She was also beginning to like him. He might be a bit too cheeky, but at least life wasn't dull when he was around. And he was funny. Mr Murray's hair *did* look as if it had been cut with a lawnmower.

"You can stay." Ms O'Grady had come back. "But you better keep those promises. Except for the one about breathing. Any more trouble and I'll personally see to it that you can't draw breath."

Was she threatening to strangle him? Rosie giggled at the image.

Mr Murray led the way through the forest park, while Ms O'Grady stayed at the back.

At first they surged forward, some of the boys racing through the forest, trying to spook each other, or climbing the trees. David Byrne hung back with a few of the girls and Ms O'Grady, trying to make friends.

"Is there a lot of wildlife here, Miss?" He asked.

"Apart from yourself, do you mean?"

He looked so crestfallen Rosie felt sorry for him. Ms O'Grady did too because she added, "There are rabbits and hares and all sorts of birds. Some foxes, I suppose and higher up you might even see falcons. Do you like animals, David?"

"They're ace, Miss. I have an alsation and a rabbit at home. They're dead funny. The alsation's called 'Rambo' but his name should be 'Custard', cos he's even afraid of the rabbit, Miss, who's called 'Kickers'. That's cos he's always kicking Rambo with his hind legs. And when they're in front of the fire, he climbs up on Rambo's back to sleep."

The boy's face was animated and Ms O'Grady was laughing.

The path was a gradual climb and suddenly, quite high up, they rounded a bend into a clearing and found themselves staring across a deep valley into Powerscourt Demesne. Far below, they could see the rolling lawns and gardens, the groves and fountains and the ruins of the old house. To their right, a waterfall tumbled down a rocky cliff.

The scene was like an old painting and if there had been ladies in long dresses on the lawns below, Rosie would not have been surprised. She was overcome by a sense of a slippage in time. If she closed her eyes she might well open them to another century.

By road, Oak Park was not far from Powerscourt and Rosie had a powerful feeling of being drawn into another world. For a moment she was dizzy and did not dare to blink. Then Mr Murray led them back through the trees and the scene was gone.

They had lunch in a sheltered sunny spot and then climbed Maulin, the unfit struggling to keep up with the rest. After they'd finished Djouce, the whole class was moaning. "Like banshees in the night," Ms O'Grady said.

"Not to worry," jollied Mr Murray as he bounded up and down the line. "Only another few miles to the hostel! Think how fit you'll be."

"We'll be flamin' dead!" Rosie said, wondering which part of her ached most.

"Not at all. By the end of the week, you'll be running up these mountains."

"We'll be running away from you. Limping, more like." David Byrne's good humour was gone. He seized Mr Murray's coat sleeve. "Can I hang on to you, Sir? Please Sir?"

Mr Murray shook him off. "Where's your spirit, boy! Stand on your own two feet."

"I can't. They're killing me! I should've gone home when I had the chance. We're all dying."

"Miserable bunch. Pay attention to what Ms O'Grady's doing. Follow her example."

They looked sourly in her direction. She was busy doing stretching exercises. Taking no notice of their glares, she smiled. "You lot should try this. Keeps your muscles supple."

"I haven't got a muscle," Rosie said bitterly, "not any more. They've all been worn away."

It was dusk by the time they hobbled into Oak Park, past the derelict gate lodge, all silent in contrast to their bubbling energy that morning. Rosie was sure she would keel over if she stopped. She could practically hear herself creak with pain.

Yet her weariness made her susceptible to atmosphere. The tall trees that lined the avenue to the big house whispered her name in the dusk. Trudging on her own along the cracked and overgrown pathways behind her classmates, she heard footsteps beside her and the light breeze carried voices. Did she imagine what they said? Was she hallucinating with exhaustion?

"Not long now, Jane. Soon we'll be able to rest."

"Oh, I hope so, Joseph. I'm very tired. There's no one else as weary in all the world."

"Wrong. I am. I'm dead tired." Rosie murmured without thinking.

"What? Who's that? Jane, did you hear someone?"

"No. It's the trees. They make me shiver, rustling and sighing."

The voices faded as they approached the house.

In the twilight it was magnificent. The ravages of time were almost erased in the fading light. The cream stone was warm and inviting. Huge steps beckoned to the wide front door, with pillars on either side. Long windows added to the splendour. Up close, Rosie could see the stone had crumbled here and there. Some of the glass was broken and the paint work around the sills was peeling.

Looking up, she saw small panes of glass in the windows of the turret rooms. She thought she detected a candle gleaming.

Inside, the floor of the hall was like a giant chessboard made of marble. And a great staircase, flanked by an oak and brass banister, curved round at each landing to sweep on to the next storey.

Mr Murray led them into a room off the hall where a welcoming fire was lit and the warden waited to greet them.

"Good evening, boys and girls." A kindly, middle aged woman, she took in their weariness.

"First, I'll show you your dormitories, then the shower rooms. You'll feel much less tired after a good wash. Later, you'll find the kitchen in the basement. Nothing like a hot meal to cheer you up. Remember, you can only use one wing of the house because that's all we've renovated so far. And don't go beyond the first floor. The rest of the building isn't safe. You'll see the warning notices. And of course, if you need anything, just ask me or the assistant warden. You will meet him tomorrow. Now, if you'll follow me . . ."

But before they did, Rosie said, "What about the turret rooms? Does anyone live up there? I thought I saw a light in one of the windows."

"Probably a trick of the twilight. Those rooms are out of bounds. They were the servants' quarters in the old days. Now the floors are collapsing in some of them. They're impossible to get into."

Joseph? Had that been his bedroom? Was he trying to tell her something – that this was her route to the past?

Impossible or not, she'd have to get up there somehow.

Some time later, after they'd washed, after they'd fried their rashers and sausages and made enough chips for an army, after they'd eaten every last morsel with the exquisite pleasure of the famished and after they'd cleared up and were gathered around the fire, then at last, Mr Murray told them the story he'd promised.

They had formed themselves into a wide circle, most of them sitting cross-legged on the floor. Mr Murray sat on one side of the fire, opposite Ms O'Grady. Rosie had her tape recorder ready. Her tutor was a wonderful storyteller, given to putting on strange accents, willing to frighten them with unexpected shrieks. His tales were always terrifying, his timing and his use of props perfect. In class he would disappear behind the desk, and emerge wearing a gruesome mask that gave them all a heart attack.

Or if he said there was a sound of ghostly knocking, this was sure to be followed by thunderous banging on the classroom door. No one would want to open it. By means of bribery and threats, Mr Murray would get some poor patsy to turn the handle. Of course, there was never anyone there. In the two months they'd known him, the teacher had scared them half to death with his stories and they were always dying for more.

Now 1E leaned towards him in anticipation.

"Towards the end of the last century," he began, "in this very house, a young boy was employed to do odd jobs and work in the gardens. He arrived out of nowhere, ragged and dirty, with his younger sister in tow. Of course he was turned away from the front door. 'If you want something, boy,' the butler told him, 'use the tradesman's entrance round the back.'

"They might have been turned away from there too, so dirty and unkempt were they, only the cook saw them. She had a kind heart and some influence in the house – her cooking being so delicious. Sneaking the boy and his sister into the laundry room, she got ready two tubs of hot water and made them scrub until they were immaculate. Then she found some cast-offs belonging to the children of the house, ready to go to charity. The clothes were not a satisfactory fit, but they were clean. Neatly dressed, hair washed, untangled and nicely combed, she sent the boy out to the head gardener with instructions that he was to find him a job. To offend the cook was to eat badly for months. Please her and your meals were fit for royalty. So the head gardener, having a healthy appetite, was delighted with this opportunity to increase the cook's happiness and promptly hired the boy. Anyway, he liked the cut of him, the way he looked him in the eye and answered his questions. And for all his thinness, the boy was tall and wiry and willing to work hard. The girl too made a good impression on the housekeeper and she was hired as scullery maid and general skivvy.

"For a while they were happy, considering themselves fortunate to have found employment at a time when the poor could quite easily starve to death. Then disaster struck. The young master of the house hated the gardener's boy for whatever reason and contrived to have him blamed for the robbery of the famous de Courcy necklace. A rare and perfect object, it had been given to Lord de Courcy when he had served in India, by his good friend, the Maharajah of Kashmir. His Lordship gave it to his wife in the early days of their marriage and it was her dearest possession.

"None of the servants believed the gardener's boy was the thief. He was well regarded by all of them. On the other hand, they knew what the young master was capable of, how vicious he could be. But there was nothing they could do.

"Without informing his mother, who by all accounts was a kindly lady, the young master sent for the constabulary. Before they arrived he sought to humiliate the boy further. Calling together all the servants, he proclaimed him a thief and lorded it over him that the police would soon arrive to arrest him. But his lordship was a little too previous. For the servants urged the gardener's boy to make his escape. This did not suit the master, who threatened them with instant dismissal. They ignored him and urged the lad to hurry.

"The boy looked at the young master with contempt and although his time was running out, he held his nerve and his voice was steady when he told him, 'Some night I shall come back for you. I shall have justice. Some night you will hear a musket shot and that will be the last thing you ever hear in this life.'"

Mr Murray stopped, taking in the absorbed faces of his class. Not a sound from any of them. This was different to his first version of Cyril's death and it was different to Gran's story, Rosie thought, but it was even more exciting. One way or another, Cyril de Courcy had had a nasty death.

"The servants parted to let the gardener's boy escape, then closed ranks when his lordship tried to follow. He cursed and ordered them to stop the lad, but they were stony-faced. Afterwards, in a rage, he had the sister dismissed. No one knows what became of either of them. Perhaps they starved to death, perhaps they found other employment. But one thing is sure, the gardener's boy kept his promise. He did come back . . . Or at least, his ghost did. And on a moonlit night like tonight, you can hear his footsteps on the stairs."

He stopped to listen. They did not have to strain to hear the sound of boots on the stairway beyond the door. There was a gasp of terror. Rosie smiled. Was she the only one who noticed Ms O'Grady wasn't with them anymore?

But the smile was wiped away when Mr Murray said softly, "And when he reaches the landing, a musket shot rings out like this . . ."

There was a huge bang and the fire flared for a few seconds.

The reaction was beyond even Mr Murray's expectations. Shrieking, the class gripped one another in terror and leapt to their feet. Their eyes on the door, they backed away from it, as if any moment something awful might enter. They did not stop screaming.

Putting on the light, Mr Murray had to roar to make himself heard. "Calm down at once, you shower of ninnies! The gardener's boy *never* said he'd come back. I made up that bit. And I threw a small firecracker into the fire. There was no musket shot."

Eventually they subsided, further relieved when Ms O'Grady came back and said she had done the footsteps on the stairs. Finally relaxed, they said:

"That was the best story I ever heard, sir!"

"It was a lovely story."

"Dead scary, sir."

"'Course I never believed any of it anyway."

At midnight, they were in their dormitories, worn out by the day.

Rosie waited till every girl was settled in her bunk.

Then she replayed the tape from where the footsteps went up the stairs. In the high ceilinged room, the sound was clear and eerie. Shushing each other, the girls' silence was tense. There was a collective moan at the musket shot. Afraid to get out of bed, each of them huddled beneath their blankets. Too terrified to speak, it slowly dawned on them that one of their number was trying to stifle uncontrollable laughter.

"It's a trick."

"Who's laughing?"

"Put on the light!"

"It's Rosie McGrath! She's got a tape recorder."

Indignantly, they bombarded her with pillows. But eventually, her mirth was infectious and they started giggling. Soon they were hysterical and Ms O'Grady arrived to restore order. For some reason, the appearance of the teacher in a perfectly normal pair of pyjamas made them worse. Patiently, she got them to settle down and soon the lights were off and one by one, they went to sleep.

Closing her eyes, Rosie wondered what had really happened in Oak Park in 1870. "I bet Joseph was just as interesting as in Mr Murray's story."

She shivered with excitement, "Tomorrow, I might get to meet him."

Chapter 3

LYING IN her bunk the next morning, Rosie was not so confident.

There were so many problems to overcome. Giving Mr Murray the slip was one. Her trip would probably take a week. To be gone for that length of time without anyone realising she was missing would take some planning. Getting back to 1870 was a major difficulty. The warden had been very insistent that upstairs was out of bounds. "The floors are collapsing," she'd told them. "In some cases only the joists are left."

Yet Rosie was certain that was where she would find Joseph. The servants had lived in the garret rooms. And she was sure she hadn't imagined the candle flickering in the window last night. It was Joseph's way of letting her know where he was.

But the thought of inching her way across dangerous floorboards, of maybe falling through them, made Rosie weak. She could injure herself and no one would know where she was. Or she might go back to the wrong year!

On her last trip she had discovered that time was like a magnet, the years vying with each other to draw her back. It would be easy to make a mistake. What if for some reason she could not return? Then she might be lost forever, in a past full of strangers. She shivered.

"Are you all right, Rosie? You look sick." It was one of her classmates, standing beside her bunk. The words gave Rosie the first part of her plan.

"I feel rotten," she said, still shivering, managing to make her teeth chatter.

When Ms O'Grady was summoned, she took one look at the girl and said, "You won't be climbing any mountains today."

"I want to go home." Rosie's voice was convincingly weak.

The teacher nodded. "That would probably be best. We'll see what Mr Murray says. One of us will have to go with you."

This was not part of Rosie's evolving plan. "There's no need," she said a little less feebly. "I can get a bus."

"Out of the question. You're not fit to travel on your own. I'll see Mr Murray."

When the teacher was gone, Rosie got dressed and went down to the kitchen. Breakfast was underway and Ms O'Grady was talking to the tutor. "One of us will have to accompany her," Rosie heard her say.

Mr Murray's face fell and Rosie guessed at once how much he'd looked forward to being with Ms O'Grady.

"I'll be all right on my own," she told them. "I don't feel faint or anything. Just a bit fluey. I'm not going to throw up on the bus."

Her tutor went slightly green. Ms O'Grady became even more concerned. "How awful for you if you did!" She said, "Not to mention all the other passengers."

"I suppose so. Vomit has a terrible smell," said Rosie, who found the topic quite interesting. "They'd have to open all the windows. Imagine being in a bus for an hour with sick all over the floor. Gross!"

Mr Murray opened his mouth and closed it again. His face was even greener and there were beads of sweat on his forehead. Rosie realised her words had made him queasy and she changed the subject. "Did you have a nice breakfast, Mr Murray?" She herself was starving, but could hardly eat if she were supposed to be sick. "I suppose you had rashers and eggs and sausages and pudding with fried bread," she said wistfully.

Her tutor stood up abruptly and opened the window, gulping in the fresh air.

Ms O'Grady was looking at her suspiciously. "How can you talk about food when you're not feeling well?"

"Mom says if I were dying I'd talk about food," she said truthfully. The teacher continued to study her and Rosie did her best to look weak. "Best not take any chances," Ms O'Grady was thinking aloud. "A hostel is no place for you if you're not well. But one of us will go with you. Definitely."

Dismayed, Rosie argued vehemently. "But why? I'm not a baby. I can get home on my own and I promise I won't vomit. I never do, not on buses. Anyway, Mr Murray can't go. He's the leader. He knows the way. And you can't go 'cos you have to stay at the back for the slow walkers. And you can't make everyone wait till one of you brings me home, 'cos it'll take nearly three hours to get to Whitehall and back. I'll be all right, I promise. Once I get home Mom will look after me."

The teachers looked at each other. The girl was right. The whole situation was very awkward. One of them could not look after a whole class on the mountains and it would not be worth while going at all if they had to delay for three hours. Yet, if only for insurance purposes, an adult had to go with the girl.

It was the warden who came up with a solution. She had been hovering in the background for the last few minutes. "It would be a pity to ruin the day, Mr Murray. I can leave young Rosie home."

Her tutor was delighted, but his face fell when Ms O'Grady said regretfully, "We can't impose on you like that. After all, you have the hostel to run."

"Well, actually, I have a meeting to attend at twelve o'clock in Mountjoy Square, which is very near where Rosie lives. It would be silly for either of you to take her when I'm going in that direction anyway. The assistant warden will look after things in my absence. He'll be here before I go."

Mr Murray and Ms O'Grady beamed at each other and at the warden. It was the perfect solution! Rosie on the other hand was dismayed.

"Isn't this wonderful, Rosie?" Mr Murray was in great form. "Now you can go home knowing you haven't ruined my day – I mean *our* day."

"I want to go on the bus. I like buses." Rosie knew she sounded ungrateful, but that was exactly how she felt.

Going home was not part of her plan. And when she got there she'd have to pretend to be sick and she'd have to stay in bed for a few days, with a thermometer stuck in her mouth, eating the kind of baby food Mom always insisted on when anyone was ill. All this misery when she should be having a marvellous adventure in the nineteenth century!

"I am not at all impressed with your attitude, Rosie." Ms O'Grady's voice was level, but her eyes had narrowed. "You have not thanked the warden for taking the trouble to bring you home."

"Thanks, Warden," Rosie muttered. Flamin' prison warden, she thought. And those two are worse. Sometimes I hate teachers!

The woman smiled benevolently. "We'll leave around ten," she said," and before we go, you can give me your telephone number and I'll ring home. It'll save time for your teachers."

"Very kind, I'm sure," Rosie said. The situation was getting worse every second. The warden nodded and went off on her rounds.

Now David Byrne intervened. He had been at the next table, listening to every word and hatching his own plans.

"Sir. Sir! I could stay. Look after Rosie until ten o'clock. Keep an eye on her. Tell the warden if she vomits."

Rosie was furious. Interfering busybody! "I don't need you to look after me. You just want to get out of climbing those mountains."

The boy looked injured and Ms O'Grady tut-tutted. "That's not nice, Rosie. David is only thinking of you." Behind the teacher's back the boy winked at her. She glared back.

Mr Murray was enthusiastic. "That's a great idea, David. I can see it's going to be a wonderful day now that Ms O'Grady and I can be together – " he reddened, "to look after the class properly."

David beamed. Rosie fumed. "I am well able to look after myself. He's only going to make me feel sicker!" Her face was red.

"You're beginning to sound like your old self," Ms O'Grady said.

Rosie closed her eyes. That boy was so aggravating. Such a pain! Just when she was beginning to like him too. But he'd be unbearable now, pretending to look after her, asking her every ten seconds did she want to vomit. Idiot!

"I have to sit down," she said feebly. "All this arguing is making me worse." She put a hand to her head and hoped she looked ill.

"I'll get you a cup of tea," David said and grinned at Rosie's poisonous look.

"Such a nice boy!" Ms O'Grady murmured. "I wouldn't have thought he could be so caring. We've misjudged him."

Rosie snorted and hastily made it a cough.

"That's settled then." Mr Murray was rubbing his hands with satisfaction. "I'll ring home this evening to see how you are."

Rosie groaned. Nothing was going according to plan.

Half an hour later, Mr Murray strode out of the hostel and off into the wilderness, singing at the top of his voice, "Keep Right on to the End of the Road." He was totally off key and 1E groaned as they followed him, ignoring his demands to "Sing up and move faster." They were still suffering from yesterday's exertions. Yet, they felt sorry for Rosie, who would miss all the fun.

"At least you'll be able to walk," they consoled her. "We'll all be on crutches by the time those two are finished with us."

"And you won't have to listen to that terrible squawking. What he calls singing."

He says he's going to teach us every verse of 'The Spaniard who Blighted my Life.' He says it's a comic song, though with him singing, it'll be tragic. For us anyway."

"Maybe you're lucky to be going home!"

They sighed, but she knew from the way they ran to catch up on their teacher, they didn't mean a word of it and were just being kind.

When they were gone, she turned to tell David Byrne exactly what she thought of his interference, but before she opened her mouth, he said, "That was flamin' brilliant, Rosie. You put on a terrific act, got the two of us out of all that climbing."

"Well I didn't want to get *you* out of it. So you needn't bother hanging around!"

"I won't. The village is supposed to have a great pool hall. That's where I'm off to. Do you have any food?"

"Food?"

"Goodies. I left all my stuff at home on the kitchen table. I thought Mom would pack it for me."

Rosie began to boil. "So, because you're too lazy to look after your own stuff, you want me to give you mine! No chance."

"It'd only be a loan. You won't need it if you're going home, will you? And I'll probably starve to death in the next few days, galloping over the hills with those two maniacs, with nothing proper like Coke and sweets to enjoy."

"Too bad. You're not having mine. Why should I hand over my crisps, chocolate and bubble gum, my fizzbags, my drinks and popcorn and especially my chocolate Kimberleys?"

Too late she realised David was licking his lips, his anticipation growing at each item.

"Because," he said simply, "I know you're up to something

and if you don't share with me, then I'm going to have to stay here, stick by you every second, look after you and make sure you don't vomit."

"*You'd* make anyone vomit!" Rosie felt vicious. "I'm not giving you all my food. You can have two things and that's all. If that doesn't satisfy you then you'll miss your pool hall and you'll get nothing."

David looked at her, calculating. "Is it a six-pack of crisps?"

"It is."

"How many bubblegums?"

"Ten sourballs."

"Right. It's a deal. I'll take the crisps and the chewing gum."

Well at least it would mean she'd have some food left for the nineteenth century. She wouldn't have to put up with fish head stew or pig's heart, as she had on her previous adventures.

In a few minutes she had brought down David's share and dumped it his feet.

He was overwhelmed. "Thanks Rosie! That's deadly. And anyway, what's the point of you just bringing it all home with you? It'll do more good here, with me." He grinned and then turned serious. "I know you don't believe me, but I'll pay you back. I promise."

Oddly enough, she did believe him.

He lifted the plastic bag. "I don't know what you're up to, but good luck anyway. I'm going down to the village after I put this away. When you see the warden, tell her I've gone to the toilet or something."

He grinned. She could not help smiling back as he waved good-bye.

Rosie went up to the dormitory and lay on the bunk. How on earth was she going to get out of this mess? All she wanted was for everyone in the hostel to think she was safe at home while she spent some time in the past. Now the warden was going to ring home before delivering her to her doorstep and Mr Murray was going to check up later. Her plan was in ruins!

Downstairs the phone rang. A few minutes later a door slammed and footsteps came running up the stairs.

"Rosie! I'm sorry, I can't take you home. I've just got a message from the assistant warden. Like yourself, he's not feeling well and won't be in. There must some bug doing the rounds. Anyway, I can't leave the hostel unattended, in case more visitors arrive. What are we going to do?"

Rosie groaned convincingly. "I want to go home. I'm not well."

"I'm sure Mr Murray won't want you giving whatever it is you have to the rest of the class. I suppose I could put you on the bus, though if you're that poorly . . . "

"Oh the bus would be great!" Rosie sat up. "The bus always makes me feel good."

"If you're sure. That would solve a lot of problems. Now it arrives at eleven o'clock. Tell that nice boy who's looking after you – where is he anyway?"

"In the toilet."

"Well, tell him to keep an eye out for the bus and to let me know when it's coming. I'll have a word with the driver so he can look after you."

Rosie groaned and lay down again.

"Don't forget to give me your phone number before you go. There's a while yet and you might as well have a little rest." Rosie put a hand to her brow and the warden tiptoed out of the dormitory.

Half an hour before the bus was due, she sneaked downstairs and scouted around for the phone. She couldn't see one. It must be in the warden's office. Rosie knocked on the door. No answer. She entered the empty room and saw the phone on the desk. Swiftly, she pulled out the connections. It was more difficult to make it look as if they hadn't been touched and it took her some frantic minutes to stuff the wire ends back under the socket. Hopefully, it would take ages to locate the fault. With any luck the phone wouldn't be fixed for days. The village was a couple of miles away and maybe Mr

Murray wouldn't think it was that urgent. It was a forlorn hope but she would have to take the risk. Rosie did not want to think about what she would do if her parents ever found out she'd been missing for days.

Collecting her bag from the dormitory, she waited in the shadows of the landing until she heard the rumble of the bus. Even at this distance it was audible. Surely the warden heard it too?

The engine slowed on the narrow road, the airbrakes swished. There was no other sound except the loud throbbing. Downstairs the warden came racing through the hall. Rosie's heart sank. Just then the bus revved up and moved on, the noise fading.

"Drat that kid! She got the bus without telling me." The warden turned towards her office, still talking to herself, "I hope the driver doesn't go too fast and make her feel worse. Still, it can't be helped now. And she never gave me her number. I'll have to look it up. Wait till that boy comes in. I'll give him a piece of my mind."

Rosie smiled. David would have a job to wriggle out of this, but she was sure he would manage somehow.

Now at last everything was going according to plan and the coast was clear.

The stairs up from the first floor was blocked by a metal bar with a large sign:

WARNING. NO ENTRY.

She slipped under and kept close to the wall. At intervals the banisters were missing and there was quite a drop to the hall. Remembering the tenement stairs – or lack of them – in 1920, Rosie felt these were safe by comparison. It was only when she began to make her way to the third floor that she grew afraid. Here the banisters were completely gone and some of the marble steps had caved in, giving the stairway a toppled, dangerous look. With her weight, would it crash down to the next floor? Gingerly she inched upwards. On the landing, rubble from the ceiling was piled up, but she could manoeuvre her way quite safely around the inside. Leaning forward a little she saw the chequered floor far below. For a moment she swayed, then felt the security of the wall behind her and knew she was in no real danger.

There had to be a stairway leading to the garret, but she could see no sign of one. It must be behind one of the landing doors. Carefully she made her way around, testing each step before giving it her full weight. Behind the third doorway she found a narrow wooden staircase that disappeared into darkness after a few steps. Here, the steps were safe and she climbed quickly.

Emerging from the blackness onto a narrow corridor, Rosie gaped. Here and there the floor was missing, light filtering up through the joists from the huge window on the landing below. Cobwebs gleamed like bits of tattered net curtains. In the shadows on the ceiling she could make out mould and crumbling plaster. She touched the wall and drew back from its dampness. Something scurried over her foot and she saw a greyish form disappear along the corridor. A rat! Chill quivers darted up her spine. Trembling with fear, she took deep breaths until her courage returned.

Where the floor was intact, it looked safe enough. Six doors, six rooms. Which one had belonged to Joseph? How would she know?

She opened the first door. A spider's web wafted against her face. Dust covered everything. Particles danced in the weak sunlight and hung from the shreds of curtains and bedcovers.

Apart from the tatters and the dust, everything was as it had been in the last century. The high iron bedstead was still there, as were the jug, washbasin, matting, cupboard. But there was nothing of Joseph.

"You've got to help me. Tell me where you are," she whispered.

Silence.

Perhaps this wasn't where she would find him at this time

of day. Perhaps he would have been working in the gardens or doing odd jobs in some other part of the house. What time was it anyway? She glanced at her watch, pressing the small light. Eleven twenty. The date was blinking at her. Was the battery going? Then she started. How stupid she was, not changing the date!

There was a kind of ritual to going back to the past and she should have remembered it from the last time.

Immediately she switched the year to 1870.

What else?

When she had wanted to travel back to 1956, she had thought of nothing but Aunt Rose. When she'd wanted to find Catherine in 1920, she had fastened on her name, calling her over and over. Now, closing her eyes, she concentrated.

"Joseph . . . Joseph . . . " she repeated the word like a chant. Then she heard a low murmur of voices, but the words were unclear.

She needed something else to bridge the distance.

Setting down her rucksack, she took from it Joseph's portrait. Earnestly she looked at his face, studying the half smiling, half serious expression. "Where are you?" she pleaded.

The voices started again, still low, but now she could hear the words.

"When I have time, Jane, I will mend the box for you."

"Thank you, Joseph. I shouldn't like Miss Florence to know I damaged her gift."

They were in the next room! In her excitement, Rosie hoisted the rucksack onto her shoulder and turned too quickly. Slipping on the damp floor, her foot went through a weak piece of timber and she fell awkwardly, making a huge racket which echoed in the empty corridor. The rucksack shunted over her head, weighing her down. Swirling dust choked her. After the first moment of shock, when her heart thudded against the wood, she hauled herself up.

Now the silence was acute. It was the silence of intent

listeners and Rosie knew they had heard her across the century, just as she had heard them.

She leaned against Joseph's door, suddenly afraid. The boy had been suspected of a crime. If she went back, she might get into trouble with the police for trying to help him. She could end up in a Victorian prison. She might never get home. And all for what? To change a past that everyone except Gran had forgotten about?

"Come in, please. The door is open." This time the voice was Jane's. Rosie remembered the story of her hard life, how she had missed Joseph so much, always wanting to clear his name. At Rosie's age she had been left to fend for herself, totally alone.

If she could change that, then it was worth a few risks.

She turned the handle and pushed. Sunlight from the small window dazzled her. She could not see, but sensed a change in atmosphere. The musty smell and heavy choking dust disappeared. An odour of cleanliness was everywhere, of disinfectant, of beeswax, of metal polish. Blinking till her eyes adjusted, she stood in the doorway, a shadowy figure, caught in the light.

Then she saw them. The boy holding a wooden box, the girl sitting on the small bed, both of them staring at her.

She stepped into the room.

Chapter 4

"WAS IT you making all that noise?" The girl asked. "Such a rumpus. We thought someone was smashing the floor."

"I was in a way," said Rosie, careless of her words, concentrating instead on the boy and girl. Joseph was tall and thin, dark trousers tucked into boots just below the knee, a brown waistcoat over a neat workman's shirt, sleeves rolled up. The girl was standing now, her long grey dress covered by a starched apron, fair hair neatly tied back. A white cap set off her dark eyes, which were staring at Rosie with disbelief.

"That's not possible," she muttered.

"Of course not, the girl is daft," Joseph said, "It would take a strong workman with a hatchet to smash those timbers."

Rosie reddened, "I fell," she said, "that's what made the noise."

The boy was scornful. "Even Mrs Smiley couldn't make that noise falling and she's as big as a battle ship! Anyway, who are you?"

"That's what I should like to establish an' all," a large voice boomed in her ear. "I been stood here gasping for the last few minutes, with not one of you paying me a bit of notice, 'cept to insult my plumpness, young Joseph!" The accent was west-country English.

Rosie turned to see a very large, red-faced, indignant woman who was still fighting for breath. She was wearing a long black dress with white collar and cuffs.

"I come up here," she heaved, "and what do I find? You two!" She pointed at the brother and sister. "Idling. Not doing your duty. And gossiping with strangers!"

Joseph opened his mouth, but the large woman was in full spate.

"And why am I here? Do you know how many steps there are in this house for my poor frail body to climb?"

Rosie giggled and Jane said hastily, "Yes Mrs Smiley. You've told us. One hundred and fifty eight – not counting the cellar which has six, or the front entrance which has ten."

"One-hundred-and-seventy-four steps! And some of them right cruel indeed. And why have I had to climb them?"

She paused dramatically. Rosie was fascinated. It was quite a number of steps. Especially for such a large woman.

"'Cos I heard a mighty ruckus!" Mrs Smiley said at last, "and thought the ceiling was about to fall on top of us, only to find the hullabaloo were caused of a slip of a stranger-girl and myself described as a battleship!"

Her tone was outraged but Rosie thought she saw a gleam of amusement in Mrs Smiley's eyes. Joseph, however, did not detect it and was full of apologies.

"It wasn't an insult, Mrs Smiley. Why me and Jane think battleships are wonderful. We've seen pictures of them in the gazette. There's no better vessel." He trailed off.

"And am I a vessel, young Joseph? Do I sail?"

For a moment Rosie could imagine the magnificent Mrs Smiley floating across the ocean. She got a fit of the giggles and at once the large woman focused on her.

"As for you, Miss Idiot! New scullery maids do not make free with their mistress's house, nor break up the floorboards when they have a mind! You better follow me. And you two, I am sure you has your duties to attend to, which are not to stand all day gossiping and insulting your betters." She swirled and glided down to the end of the narrow corridor. Rosie followed.

Mrs Smiley stopped at another door. "This here's your room."

Rosie took in the sloping ceiling, bare floorboards and the high iron bedstead. There was a kind of dresser with an enamel jug and basin and a small press.

"The po is under the bed," Mrs Smiley said, "to be emptied every morning round the back in the po pit afore you start your duties at six o'clock. Young Jane will show you.

"Now the cupboard is small, but I daresay it will accommodate whatever it is you've brought in that very peculiar bag of yours. I see you have your uniform already. Did Mr Harvey fetch it for you?"

Rosie looked at her blankly, then glancing down, realised she was dressed exactly like Jane. Touching her head, she found the small hat and grimaced.

"Mr Harvey! The butler. Don't pull faces, girl, and straighten up that mob-cap. You've made it all askew!"

Rosie took off the hat and looked with distaste at the puffy crown, the broad band and the frills. Gross! But it had to be worn and she settled it on properly while Mrs Smiley watched her, eyes narrowed.

"One of the Brannigan girls, ain't you? I thought you weren't coming for another week on account of being sick an' all. What's your name?"

"Rosie."

"Well, Rosie, I'm glad you're better and obviously eager to do your duty. Your mother can do with the five pound wages, having all those mouths to feed."

Shocked into indignation, Rosie said, " Five pounds a week! Is that all?"

"Five pound a week! Don't be ridiculous! A good *sensible* girl, I were told. Nobody mentioned 'feeble minded with daft notions'. Lady de Courcy pays five pound a year to scullery maids and that's *far* beyond what's expected."

"Of course," Rosie said, recovering "I meant a year. Very generous, I'm sure. And what do I have to do to earn this huge amount?"

Mrs Smiley looked at her sharply and frowned, but the girl's face was innocent of sarcasm.

"What you have to do is what every other skivvy has to do. Rise at six, help in the kitchen, sweep and scrub floors, wash dishes, polish, mop, run errands and clean where ever and whatsomever Cook and me requires. Keep well out of the way of the gentry, especially young master Cyril. He cannot abide grubby servants."

Outraged, Rosie said, "But I'm not a bit grubby!"

"Not yet, you're not. But you will be. That's if you're doing your duties properly. Apron should rightly be filthy at the end of the day. And that's another thing. No matter how late you finish, even after midnight you must leave your cap and apron down to the laundry for washing and you must collect your clean uniform for the next day. Undergarments you may wash yourself in the basin provided."

Rosie groaned. This was a nightmare.

Mrs Smiley frowned. "Stop moaning, girl. No looks of misery. I were told Mrs Brannigan were delighted for her daughter to have a position here. A step up for the family, I were told. Indoor servants have prospects, girl, even a scullery maid. But not miserable groaning scullery maids, what don't know how lucky they be! Take note girl. Work hard and be cheerful. Not a lot to ask."

Rosie managed a weak smile. It's slavery, she thought. At home, housework was not her strong point. Even putting the dishes in the dishwasher had always required an effort. Taking them out afterwards was exhausting. Now she had landed herself in a place where work was done at a lunatic rate for lunatic wages which she'd never even see. And she was expected to smile as well!

Under the housekeeper's sharp eye she stretched her mouth wide in what she hoped was a beam. Startled, Mrs Smiley said, "Are you feeling all right, girl? You're not in pain?"

"No." Rosie gritted her teeth behind the wide smile.

"Do you wish to attend to any needs before setting off on your duties?"

The girl looked blank and the housekeeper pointed at the bed.

"Oh thank you!" Rosie said, "I could do with a rest. It's been a very exhausting morning so far."

"Exhausting! Don't be ridiculous, girl. You haven't even started yet. Such daft notions. I weren't referrin' to the bed. I were referrin' to the po underneath it!"

"You were? Oh right. No, I don't need to use it just at the moment."

"Well then, you come with me girl."

Rosie did her skivvy's smile and Mrs Smiley winced. She turned to descend the back stairs, muttering, "That girl ain't all there in my opinion and I hopes she ain't demented."

Rosie stopped smiling and followed her all the way down to the basement kitchen. The housekeeper stopped at the door, some of her bustling confidence evaporating. "Now remember, girl, you be careful with Cook. She can be right crotchety!"

She knocked and a voice bellowed "Come in at once, for heaven sake!"

Mrs Smiley entered, Rosie behind her.

"Mrs Biddle, the new scullery maid. Mrs Brannigan's girl – Rosie."

Mrs Biddle wiped her hands on an immense white apron and sniffed. "Not a bit like a Brannigan! Where's your red hair girl? Girl!"

Rosie was gazing at the kitchen in awe and didn't hear the question. The whitewashed ceiling and walls contrasted with the gleaming black slate floor. Near the deep ceramic sink was a huge kitchen table and sitting on a platter was the largest piece of beef Rosie had ever seen. Shining copper pots and pans hung against the wall, near an oak dresser with delph of every description, patterned with peacocks and flowers and Chinese figures. On the floor was a large open box filled with what looked like salt. There were silver coffee pots and teapots and utensils Rosie had never seen before. Sunlight poured through the high windows. But what most attracted her gaze was the huge glowing range which added warmth to the large room.

"Girl! Is she deaf, Mrs Smiley? Am I to be ignored in my own kitchen?"

Startled, Rosie at last looked at the red-faced cook.

"I'm sorry. I wasn't listening."

Mrs Biddle's face looked as if might burst with rage, but before she could say a word, Rosie went on "It's such a beautiful kitchen! So warm! And everything is lovely. It's . . . It's . . ." she sought for the right words, "It's a work of art. That's what it is."

Cook's face was at once transformed. Her fury vanished, her colour died down and she almost smiled.

"A girl after my own heart," she said, "one who knows a true artist. I'd never have expected it of a Brannigan. Still, where there's so many children, one of them is bound to have a few brains."

"I shall leave the girl with you, Cook." Mrs Smiley said, "If you'd be so kind as to show her duties." She vanished.

There was a delicious smell of baking and Rosie spied scones cooling on a griddle on the range. She was starving. Cook caught the direction of her gaze. "Are you hungry, Rosie? Well, of course you are, coming from such a large family. How many brothers and sisters have you? Twelve is it?"

Rosie nodded, her eyes on the scones.

"It's a wonder you're so tall. I heard all the Brannigans were on the small side. Runts, most of them."

Rosie was five foot four. The Brannigans must be all leprechauns, she thought. Cook was not very tall either, though quite large and while Mrs Smiley was very wide, she definitely wasn't tall. So far the only tall person she'd met was Joseph.

"Sit down at the table, child, and have some vittles before you start. We need to nourish that brain of yours."

She put a plate of steaming scones in front of Rosie, a dish of ridged butter, a knife and a mug of creamy milk. Rosie ate everything, her eyes round with enjoyment.

"Those are beautiful scones, Mrs Biddle, the most beautiful I've ever had." Rosie always thought this about the last meal she'd eaten, unless it was truly horrible like fishhead stew. But Mrs Biddle was not to know this and she looked gratified.

Cook bustled around. Beside Rosie on the table was a parcel and Rosie idly read aloud the large label above the address. "Arnotts & Company, Henry Street, Dublin. Specialists in Exotic silks and Chinese porcelain and quality goods."

Pondering the fact that Arnotts was still there over a hundred-and-twenty-years later, Rosie did not see Mrs Biddle's expression. She cleared the last crumbs from her plate and brought her dishes over to the sink. When she turned around she thought the woman was having some sort of seizure.

"You've gone pale, Mrs Biddle – and you're staring. Are you feeling weak?"

She rushed over and helped Mrs Biddle to a chair. "What's wrong?"

"You!" Cook gasped, "You! You can read! It's not right."

Rosie knew at once she had put her foot in it and cursed herself.

Mrs Biddle gabbled on. "Mr Harvey, the butler, can read, and Miss Payne, the governess and Mrs Smiley a bit – though she lets on to read more than she can. Myself, I can make out only a word or two. And none of the other servants in the house can manage much more. And I have never heard of a Brannigan who could read! Brannigans don't go to school and have no brains. They know very little from what I've heard."

Rosie was glad she wasn't a Brannigan. By now she would've been mortified at all the insults.

Mrs Biddle's face was a shade of beetroot and getting redder in an effort to understand.

"I don't remember when I learned to read," Rosie was truthful. "Mom . . . Mother . . . says I was always looking at signs and notices on shops when I was small, trying to make them out. Then one day when I was about six, suddenly I could."

Cook digested this. "You taught yourself, that's what it is." She looked at her with envy, "Reading is a wonderful gift. You'll get on well in the world, dear."

It was Rosie's turn to stare. Then Cook lowered her voice and said hesitantly, "I get letters, Rosie, from my brother George in Boston. He got a chance of schooling a few years ago, after the great American War."

"What war?"

"The war about slaves," Mrs Biddle was impatient, "Five years ago. Everyone knows about it. Anyway, George learned to read and write and now he sends me letters. Only I can't make them out. I don't like to ask Mr Harvey and Mrs Smiley might put in what wasn't there 'cos she wouldn't admit not knowing the words."

"I could read them for you," Rosie said, "and I could write back for you!"

"Could you? Oh Rosie, would you? I never thought of writing back. But he's my only brother and I'd love to let him know I got his letters." Cook was beside herself with happiness and seized the girl's face in her two hands and planted a couple of smacking kisses on her forehead.

Rosie went beetroot and hoped Mrs Biddle didn't make a habit of kissing. Life was going to be difficult enough.

Chapter 5

"WHY, MRS Biddle! Cosseting the skivvies. So heart warming."

Everything about the woman in the doorway was thin – her smile, her bony figure, even the material of her black dress with its high collar. Her thin hair was drawn back into a severe bun, and she patted it now as she relished Cook's embarrassment.

Stepping into the kitchen, she pointed at the row of gleaming brass bells on the wall over the dresser. "I believe we have been ringing from the schoolroom for the last five minutes. It is time for Miss Florence's morning milk. But no doubt a skivvy is more important than Lady de Courcy's daughter."

The girl was furious. The woman spoke in an exaggerated drawl, as though a posh accent was somehow superior. She was so insulting! And poor Cook looked as if she'd done something wrong instead of something kind.

"I'm no skivvy," Rosie told the startled woman. "We didn't hear any bell and you're very rude to Mrs Biddle."

Cook gaped. So did the woman. Cook recovered first. Really, the girl was right. That one had a nerve! Still, Rosie should be careful. "It'd be better if you didn't speak to Miss Payne like that," she advised. "She's Miss Florence's governess and she has influence. So she says, anyway."

She turned to Miss Payne, "We heard no bell. Maybe you

didn't ring it. Maybe you preferred to come nosying down here."

The woman was breathing hard. "Your kitchen would not entice any lady!"

Cook kept her cool. "Miss Payne is from London," she told Rosie. "It's another world, as she keeps telling us poor servants. A *civilised* world. Persons from London are better than the rest of us. Miss Payne will tell you so herself. Won't you, dear?"

Rosie recognised sarcasm when she heard it. There was no love lost between Cook and the governess, a fact that made her bolder. "Well, it's not civilised to look down on people," she told Mrs Biddle. "I think her name suits her."

Cook smiled, but Rosie had gone too far. The governess gripped her arm, squeezing tightly, and pulled her close.

"That is no way to speak to your betters, you wretched, wretched girl. Such impertinence will not be tolerated by Lady de Courcy. When she is informed, you will have to leave this house at once. And if I have my way, you will not be engaged by any family in Wicklow. You do not know your place!"

Mrs Biddle planted herself between them, a difficult feat for such a large lady in such a small space. Miss Payne was forced to release Rosie and step back.

"Now, Miss High and Mighty," Cook said, "You'd best tell Lady de Courcy that if this girl goes, I go too. She won't thank you, for there isn't another cook as good in the whole county."

Miss Payne knew she was beaten and shot Rosie a venomous look. "That skivvy will not go unpunished. Now, have Miss Florence's milk and biscuits sent up to the schoolroom without delay. I have important business to attend to." She stalked out.

"I can't abide that woman," Cook said. "She has a miserable appetite and cannot tell the difference between fine cuisine and lumpen stodge." She busied herself with the schoolroom tray, adding, "You've made an enemy there, child. But then, she doesn't think much of any servant. And sure what else is she herself? And don't you get so upset at being called a skivvy. It's what you are, though we never had one before that could read and write. Now take this up the back stairs to the schoolroom. It's on the second floor, facing you on the landing."

Rosie had no idea how to knock on a door and open it while holding a tray, so when she got to the door marked "Schoolroom" she gave it a couple of kicks.

"Come in."

"Sorry, I can't."

The girl in the pink taffeta dress who opened the door clapped her hands. "Oh, marvellous! I am *so* hungry. Put it down on this table."

Rosie did as she was told, then stood staring. The schoolroom was bright and airy, with rugs scattered on the polished floor.

Bemused, Florence watched as the new scullery maid went over to her book case.

Rosie loved reading and the richly bound volumes on the shelves made her forget caution.

"Your books are lovely," She told Florence, examining the leather covers with their gilt lettering and gold-edged pages. "*Oliver Twist* . . . *A Chrismas Carol*. I read them. *The Poetical Works of Mr Oliver Goldsmith* . . . *A Golden Treasury of Verse* . . . *A hundred Ways Towards the Improvement of Young Ladies*. – I bet that's a riot. And this one – *Etiquette for an Empire*. Oh look at this! *Jane Eyre*."

At last a well-loved book. "*Jane Eyre* is deadly, isn't it?" She turned to the younger girl who looked at her blankly.

"Have you not read it yet?" Rosie said.

"Yes . . . eh . . . have you?" She spoke apologetically, as if the question might be out of order, but Rosie was too carried away to notice.

"Oh yes! It's one of my favourite books. I've read it twice."

Moving over to the large map on the wall, she did not see Florence's astounded expression.

"Why is almost a quarter of the world marked in red?"

"Because it belongs to the British Empire."

"That's an awful lot of countries. India . . . Australia . . . New Zealand . . . Canada . . . parts of Africa . . . Ireland." Beside the map, she noticed a vaguely familiar portrait of a large cold-eyed woman. "This isn't your mother, is it?"

The girl was startled. "That's Queen Victoria. Our great sovereign."

"She's shocking grumpy looking isn't she? Maybe she had a pain in her tummy when this was done."

From the look on Florence's face, Rosie thought it better to change the subject, and glancing at her desk she saw her next topic. "Can I see your slate? Were you doing Maths?"

Wordlessly, mouth open, Florence handed her the slate. On it was a long division sum, many of the numbers fudged or crossed out in Florence's desperate attempt to get it right.

"It's all wrong, isn't it? Oh dear, Miss Payne won't be a bit pleased. She spends ages trying to teach me mathematics, but it's no good. I'm a duffer." The girl was almost tearful.

"It must be terrible to have Miss Payne as your teacher and be the only one in her class," Rosie said.

"She's very kind generally." The girl sighed. "Only sometimes she does get awfully impatient when I don't understand what she's told me a hundred times."

"I'll try this for you," Rosie said. She was wiping the slate with her sleeve till Florence handed her a damp sponge. With a clear black surface she began to work.

"55543 divided by 67." Deftly she covered the slate. After a few pauses and alterations, she presented Florence with the solution. "There," she said, "it must be right. It comes out even. The answer is 829."

"That is wonderful. She gave me one more. I have to square 75."

"Oh, that's dead easy. The answer is 5625."

"How did you do that? You didn't even work it out."

"It's something Dad – someone – showed me. A kind of trick. If you have to square any number ending in 5, the answer ends in 25. So what you do is, take the number before the 5, multiply it by the next number in line and put 25 beside it at the end. You had to square 75. Seven multiplied by eight – the next number in line – equals 56, so your answer is 5625. Try it yourself. What's 35 squared?"

The girl worked it out slowly. "3 multiplied by 4 equals what? 12 isn't it?" Rosie nodded and Florence was jubilant. "So 1225 is the answer! You must be a genius. Wait till I show Miss Payne. I don't know how you do it!" Florence's admiration was genuine and Rosie basked in it.

"That's something I should like to know too," said a cool voice behind them.

Rosie turned to find an elegant youthful woman in a blue silk dress, staring at her.

"I like sums," Rosie said, "and once you get the hang of them they're easy."

The woman was even more puzzled. "What has hanging to do with division and multiplication? And you haven't answered my question."

Rosie was puzzled. "You mean, how did I do the sums? Here, I'll show you."

She wiped out the slate and started on the long division once again, earnestly explaining each step. "See 67 won't go into 55, so you've got to take the first three numbers – "

"That is not what I mean!" Lady de Courcy almost stamped her foot. "I know how to do it. But you! You are the kitchen maid. Mrs Smiley told me of your arrival. Usually, I greet kitchen maids at Christmas and on special feast days. Otherwise they tend to be kept out of the way, their duties generally below stairs. Therefore I know little about them. But I *do* know we have never had one who could do complicated long division sums!"

"Oh," Rosie said, abruptly realising what the problem was.

"And Mother! She can read. She has read *Jane Eyre* twice. She is a genius."

Rosie smiled at Florence. "Genius" was nice.

In school she had been described as many things by her teachers: "Loud." "Easily distracted." "Non-stop chatterbox." But never "Genius."

She remembered a report from Miss Graham, the sixth class teacher in her last school. "Rosie would make a good astronaut, as she seems mostly to inhabit another planet."

"Genius" was much nicer.

With a shock she realised Lady de Courcy was still waiting for an answer. Rosie did the only thing possible. "It's not my fault I can read and write and do sums. Everyone's always attacking me over it. But I can't help it. Anyway, I don't see why kitchen maids shouldn't read and write. Mrs Biddle says it's a gift! I shouldn't be getting into trouble over it."

There was a long silence. Then Lady de Courcy put a hand on her arm, "You're quite right, my dear. Everyone ought to be literate. When my husband was alive we spent so much time trying to persuade my tenants to send their children to school. But they do not see the value and prefer to have them working. It is *so* shortsighted. But you are an example to them all and I shall tell your mother so. What is your name?"

"Rosie. Rosie Brannigan. Did Mrs Smiley not tell you?"

"She may have done. I don't recall."

Skivvies are not important enough to bother about, Rosie thought.

Catching the look of resentment on the girl's face, her employer immediately guessed the cause. For some reason she felt guilty. This young kitchen maid seemed to expect more of her. Without meaning to, Lady de Courcy found herself explaining, "There was a time when I knew the names of everyone who worked for us, of every person who lived on the estate, but since Lord de Courcy's death I find it difficult . . ."

She trailed off.

Florence warmly continued her mother's defence.

"Managing a large estate is not easy," she said. "After Father's death in a hunting accident, Mother wasn't well and lost all interest, didn't you, Mother?"

"I certainly did *not* lose interest." Lady de Courcy was indignant. "Perhaps I lost a little heart after your father's death. Life wasn't the same. But I see I shall have to start afresh, when my own daughter thinks I do not care."

Florence was about to protest, but Lady de Courcy felt there had been enough talk in front of Rosie. Turning to her, she said, "Well, my dear, I shall make a point of commending you to your mother on Sunday, the tenants' visiting day."

That'd be a big surprise for Mrs Brannigan, Rosie thought, and one she didn't wish to be around for.

Lady de Courcy was smiling at her and she smiled back. Then she realised she was expected to be on her way. "Oh," she said, "I suppose I'd better get on with my skivvying. Right then. See you two later."

As she closed the door she heard Lady de Courcy say, "What a peculiar girl. She did not curtsy once!" Rosie eavesdropped. "You'd imagine she'd know how to curtsy. After all she knows how to read and write. But I declare, it didn't even occur to her. And it passes belief that she is one of the brainless Brannigans. That family are famous for their idiocy."

Curtsy! Rosie boiled. For five pounds a year you were expected to have a non-stop smile, slave from morning to night *and* curtsy!

Rosie did an exaggerated dip and repeated it all down the corridor. Brooding on the injustice of the nineteenth century, she did not watch where she was going. She found herself in a passage she hadn't seen before. There were no windows. Trying to remember the way she'd come, she realised she'd no idea even what floor she was on, or what direction to take. The mahogany panelling on the walls added to the darkness and made progress slow.

Leaning against the wood to rest, she was startled when a section gave way. A whole panel shifted to reveal a passageway, dimly lit by one small window. The space was narrow, about twelve feet in length. At the end of it was a door. Taking a deep breath, Rosie went through the panel.

A few steps took her to the door. She turned the heavy knob and pushed. No movement. Using all her weight and strength she shoved. This time it creaked open and cautiously, Rosie peered around.

She was staring at a large bedroom. Two long windows faced south, overlooking the front lawns, filling the chamber with daylight. Between them stood a dressing table. A fire blazed in the huge hearth, the dancing flames reflected on the highly polished floor. Dark red wallpaper and oriental rugs added to the warmth. But what dominated the room and fascinated Rosie was the four-poster bed. Its white damask curtains were tied back to reveal plump pillows and a luxurious quilt. Rosie made for it immediately.

She had to hoist herself onto the quilt, then she stretched out, head on the pillows. Her feet did not reach even three quarters way down. A seven foot giant would have found the bed quite comfortable. This was not a servant's room.

She sat up and rolled off the bed. On the dressing table were some beautiful glass perfume bottles, a silver-backed brush and comb set and some letters and cards.

Rosie lifted a gilt-edged invitation and studied it. The name jumped at her. *Lady de Courcy*. All the correspondence was for her. What luck! This was her room she had stumbled into.

I must see her necklace! Rosie thought. She wanted to hold in her hands the diamonds which had caused so much misery.

Where would Lady de Courcy keep them? Not on the dressing table anyway. Gingerly she opened the large drawer and found a dark blue velvet box. A small gold key was in the lock. Obviously the owner had no fear of thieves. Opening the box, Rosie saw bracelets and rings set into neat grooves. And on one side, in an indented space, was a small matching velvet pouch.

She pondered. So, no one yet had taken the necklace. That much was obvious. Otherwise there would have been a great hullabuloo. Instead everyone was going about their normal business. The drama had yet to unfold.

Lifting out the pouch, she spilled the diamonds into her hand. The cascade sparkled in the morning light. Three rows of perfect jewels with a centre piece as large as a twopence.

It was beautiful, yet Rosie shivered at the hard glitter of the stones and hastily she put them back.

Hearing footsteps approach, she closed the drawer and dashed back the way she had come, realising the "door" was actually a bookcase on the bedroom side. No wonder it was so hard to push! Now she hauled at the knob and the shelves creaked into place.

Back in the corridor, she closed the wooden panel behind her. Scrutinising it, she saw the decoration was different to the other panels. It had a large carved rose where the rest had vine leaves. Pressing the centre of the flower she was not really surprised to find the section moving again. Now she knew its secret and once more pulled it into place.

Rosie had only moved a few steps when she heard a murmured conversation and groped her way along the dark corridor until the voices were clearer. They came from behind a door slightly ajar. About to knock, she heard a woman mention Joseph. It was Miss Payne. She paused.

"You are right, Master Cyril. He is sly."

A petulant languid male voice replied, "He and his sister are a most unpleasant influence on Florence. Why, only yesterday she told me servants were just as good as the de Courcys. Apparently, they have the same feelings." He sniffed with incredulity.

"I do not like saying it, Master Cyril, but your sister is weak-minded. At eleven years of age she should have more wit. She should be aware of her position."

"Exactly, Miss Payne. But that fellow and his sister have wormed their way into her affections. He has even fooled my mother so that she thinks more of him than she does of me, her own son." His tone simmered with resentment.

There was silence, then Miss Payne said, "If only we could show them up in a bad light. Then Lady de Courcy would see them in their true colours."

"My thoughts precisely. My dear Miss Payne, you are a kindred spirit. My one ally in this house. I have a plan, but it requires your assistance. Without you it will fail. Will you help?"

Miss Payne simpered agreement and Cyril went on. "My sister will not speak to me because she says I insult her friends. Friends! But you are often in her room and could quite easily take the gold locket my father gave her – "

Miss Payne gasped and Cyril reassured her. "You will merely be borrowing it. Florence will have it back, once it has been found in the possession of that pup, Joseph. I shall accomplish that myself, but your part is invaluable."

Flattered, the governess declared, "What a clever plan. And if the boy goes, his sister goes also. Oh, I've noticed the looks that girl gives me. Impertinent trollop!"

Rosie had had enough. She burst into the room. "You're evil!" she shouted. "I heard every word and I'm going to tell your mother." This last she addressed to a tall fair young man leaning against the windowsill. He wore a silver grey suit, and across the front of his white shirt she could see the gold chain of a fob watch. He would have been good-looking except for his sneering expression.

"Who is this creature, Miss Payne?"

Rosie wished the high starched collar of his shirt would choke him.

"No one. Just a skivvy." But Miss Payne looked worried.

Languidly, Cyril advanced on Rosie. She backed away slightly and glared at him. "I'm not afraid of you. Your mother will listen to me."

He laughed. "And what will you tell her? You have no proof this conversation ever took place. Miss Payne and I shall deny it. There is no point in you talking to Lady de Courcy."

He was right. Or was he? "There is if that locket disappears after I've told her what I heard. She'll believe me then. Your mother and sister know you hate Joseph."

She spoke with more conviction than she felt. Cyril looked at Miss Payne who had gone pale.

"Master Cyril, I cannot afford to lose my position here."

"Of course not. It was a foolish idea, better forgotten." He bowed to her, pushed Rosie aside and sauntered down the corridor.

Miss Payne wrung her hands. "You wretched girl! Why do you interfere? You do not even know that boy and his sister." She gripped Rosie's arm and her voice rose. "Nor do you know what it is to be a governess in a household like this, where I am neither fish nor fowl! If I lose Florence's affection, I lose everything. No more requests for my company. No more confidences. No more gifts."

Rosie thought the governess had gone a little crazy. She was shaking her so violently that her teeth chattered and she could not prize herself free. "You!" Miss Payne snarled. "You have the other servants. They do not like me. I am too educated, too superior for their taste. You have your family, such as they are. I have no one except Florence. You are trying to ruin me!"

The words exploded in a tirade that left Rosie speechless. Then Miss Payne was gone like a whirlwind. Well, thank heavens that was over! She rubbed her bruised arm. What was the woman on about? At least Cyril's plot was foiled. For a moment Rosie felt triumphant. Then she remembered the diamonds and knew they would try again. She had to warn Joseph. That's if she ever found her way out of this stupid place. She hadn't a clue which direction to go.

Peering up the corridor, she felt totally lost. Then she jumped with terror when a figure loomed out of the darkness and a voice boomed, "Where've you been, girl? And why are you stuck here staring into space?"

Chapter 6

IT WAS Mrs Smiley, the housekeeper.

"I took a wrong turning and lost my way."

"You've been gone nearly two hours. As far as I can see you must have spent most of it staring at nothing. Mrs Biddle is all of a flutter worrying about you. Do you know what that means, girl?" She paused and obviously expected an answer, so Rosie shook her head.

The housekeeper sighed. "When Cook gets worried, it means her cooking don't taste so good, which upsets the whole household and life ain't quite so smooth. And all because one little skivvy wants to spend her time doting in the dark! What have you to say for yourself?"

Rosie, who had just thought of something else, seized the pause to ask a question. "Do you know anything about a secret panel, Mrs Smiley?"

"Well, I declare, your head is addled. Secret panel indeed. Stuff and nonsense. Now you just follow me – that's if you can tear yourself away from dreamland!"

"But Mrs Smiley, just in case I get lost again. Can you tell me where exactly we are now?"

"First sensible question. We are in the short corridor. When you came out of the schoolroom, you must have turned right, gone down the next set of steps, turned left, gone up a few steps, then turned left again down here. Now please, follow me. Cook will be having hy-sterics!"

Rosie followed the gliding figure, memorising the directions. Secret panels were not ordinary everyday things and she did not want to forget where this one was.

It was the servants' lunch time when they reached the kitchen, but she had no time to eat. After her initial sigh of relief at the girl's reappearance, Cook told her she must catch up on her chores.

"But I'm very hungry, Mrs B." She saw the raised eyebrows of the distinguished-looking gentleman at the top of the table and noticed that he seemed to be dressed for a dinner party with a black tux and trousers and a starched shirt like Cyril's.

The other servants were gaping at her. Cook hustled her into a back room. "Now, Rosie, I know you can read and write, but if you want to keep this job, you shouldn't aggravate Mr Harvey. See, it's your place as a kitchen maid to say nothing."

"But – "

"*But nothing*, Rosie. Otherwise you will lose your place. Now, Miss Payne wants you to bring two buckets of coal up to the schoolroom. Then she wants you to polish the oil lamp for her, trim the wick and clean out the chimney."

This was too much. It was bad enough slaving for five pounds a year. It was worse having to smile all the time. It was gross not being allowed to say anything. But on top of all that she was now expected to clean chimneys! Miss Payne was vicious.

"I am not a flamin' chimney sweep!" She burst out. "If Miss Payne wants a nice chimney, she can clean it herself!"

"Rosie! If you go on like this you won't last the day. Who said anything about being a sweep? It's the oil lamp chimney I'm talking about." Seeing the girl's blank expression, she was patient. "It's not fair expecting you to know about such things. I suppose your poor mother can only afford candles. Go and fetch the coal from the cellar." She indicated a door in the alcove, "and when you come back from the schoolroom, I'll show you how to tackle the oil lamp."

She bustled out and before Rosie could move, Jane had slipped into the alcove.

"I hope you didn't think me and Joseph were unfriendly this morning."

Why was she whispering? "Not at all." Rosie said in her normal voice. Their meeting was hours ago and she could not remember the conversation.

"Don't talk so loud," Jane pleaded. "Mr Harvey might hear. He doesn't like the servants gossiping when they have a task to do. You'll get into trouble. I only wanted to say we're much nicer, me and Joseph, than you might have thought this morning.You gave us a bit of a fright when you made all that noise." She smiled and at once her features were bright and merry instead of anxious. Rosie grinned, liking her instantly.

"Do you think we could be friends?" Jane whispered and her great-great-grandchild, anxious to show off, boomed, "Of course we can be friends!"

Jane stared at Rosie, shocked. Then, catching her new friend's mischievous expression, she got a fit of the giggles. Close to hysteria herself after her eventful morning, Rosie did the same. Not the half smothered snorts of her companion, but almost shrieks. Watching her, the tears rolled down Jane's face. If she stayed any longer, Mr Harvey would be in, demanding an explanation. She rushed away, while Rosie leaned against the wall, trying to recover.

In the kitchen, Cook hustled Jane into her seat. Mr Harvey rose to investigate the braying noise that was coming from the back room, but sat down again when Mrs Biddle said, "I hate when anyone lets a perfectly good meal grow cold. It upsets me terrible."

Picking two of the metal buckets from the alcove, Rosie made her way down the cellar steps. In the dim light from the open door, she saw the scoop and started filling the buckets. The coal was extremely dusty and soon there was a layer on her white apron. Then her mob cap fell off. She had to root around to find it. Dusting it off, she put it back on, loosening her hair in the process. She tucked the strands behind her ears and left her face quite black. Wiping her hands on the apron, she struggled up the steps with the buckets.

Emerging in a cloud of coal dust, back stooped, Rosie made her way through the kitchen and wondered why there was complete silence. Maybe none of the servants was allowed say anything at lunchtime. Maybe that was a condition of their employment and only higher up servants like Cook and Mr Harvey were let speak.

It took such an effort to carry the coal she could not look up, missing the open mouths around the table as the black cloud went past, leaving a trail of filthy footsteps on the immaculate floor.

Rosie was already on her way up the back stairs when Mr Harvey found his voice. "That skivvy looks like a coal miner. She has ruined your kitchen, Mrs Biddle and is not fit to keep her position."

The other servants were wondering why Cook hadn't thrown one of her fits and couldn't believe it when she stood up for the girl. "I won't have poor Rosie criticised. She will learn soon enough how things are done. And you shouldn't call her a skivvy, Mr Harvey. She doesn't like it."

Unused to taking any account of skivvies' likes and dislikes, the butler had another attack of speechlessness.

Once more Rosie kicked on the schoolroom door. She felt her arms had stretched to twice their normal length from the weight of the buckets. Was no one going to answer? She was just aiming her boot again when Miss Payne swung the door open. The governess screamed, more in fright at the mad-looking creature in front of her than the kick to her shin. Pain and terror turned to anger when she realised it was Rosie. "How dare you kick me, you dirty little savage?"

Rosie narrowed her eyes but said nothing. She must not lose her job till she had accomplished her mission and stopped the robbery of the necklace. Still, it was a lot to put up with.

Abruptly she put the buckets down. Miss Payne could carry them in herself.

"Come back, you stupid girl! At once! You must fill the coal scuttle and settle the fire. It has nearly gone out."

But Rosie had disappeared. Furious, Miss Payne was tempted to ring the bells till they jangled madly in the kitchen. But they might freeze to death before that dratted girl returned. There was nothing for it but to tend to the buckets herself.

In the kitchen lunch was over and the servants were gone. When Rosie came in, Mrs Biddle, hands on hips, stared at her.

"What?" said Rosie.

"You haven't looked at yourself, have you? Why you were so worried about being a chimney sweep I don't know. You can get just as dirty without ever going near a chimney!"

"Here, look." She held a looking glass up to the girl's face and Rosie saw the wild hair, black face and streaked cap. How on earth had she got so filthy?

"Wash your hands and face, girl. You're an awful ninny for one so clever." She pointed to the sink. It took Rosie a few moments to get the hang of the pump and swing the handle up and down until the water gushed out. She washed her face and hands with hard yellow soap.

Cook was proud of her sink. "You're lucky not to have to wash outside. You'd have all the lads laughing at you. This is the only room in the house with proper water. Not even her ladyship's chamber has a sink. Lord de Courcy had the pipes brought in from the well outside. He died before the rest of the house was done, poor man, and her ladyship had no heart to finish it."

She ushered Rosie into the back room and showed her how to clean the oil lamp, with a duster for the glass and metal polish for the surround. Pointing out the mantle, she lifted it off to trim the wick, then showed her where to pour in the oil and how to clear the chimney of grit, so there would be no clogging.

The operation took nearly half an hour, during which time Rosie gave thanks again and again to whoever invented the nice clean *instant* light switch. When the lamp was ready she left it outside the schoolroom, knocked and ran. She did not want to face Miss Payne.

Back with Mrs Biddle there were another half a dozen lamps to clean, then dishes to dry, floors to mop, copper to polish, potatoes and apples to peel, the big deal table to scrub, cutlery to shine and the dresser to tidy. Rosie was exhausted, but she could see that the other servants too were rushed off their feet. Mrs Biddle supervised a small army who were busy baking batches of loaves, roasting meat, cooking vegetables, preparing desserts, all of which Cook tested rigorously, giving any careless underling a smart rap on the head.

The bells in the kitchen rang constantly for "My Lady's Bedroom," or "My Lord's Dressing-room" or the "Dining-room" or "Miss Payne's room," or the "Front Sitting-room."

All over the house there was a constant demand for hot water, a bath for Lady de Courcy, basins for cleaning, a pitcher for Miss Payne, demanded with the aggrieved message that her hands were filthy from hauling coal and lighting oil lamps. Cook looked at Rosie when she heard this, but the girl's face was blank with tiredness.

The grooms and stable lads ate in the refectory, a large room at the back of the house. Cook helped Rosie set the table for them and some of the girl's weariness disappeared as they talked. Cook explained that these were regarded as live-ins as they were quartered in the stable yard near the house and were unmarried. They did not eat in the kitchen with the indoor staff as there was no room. Patiently she answered Rosie's questions. Married men had cottages on the estate and their wives were expected to look after them. Married women were generally not employed on their own but as part of a couple. For instance, Annie, the laundress, was married to the head gardener, and Lily, who managed the dairy, was the coachman's wife. They had cottages.

Rosie was puzzled by the set up. "What about you and Mrs Smiley? Who are you married to? Where do you live?"

"Whatever gave you the idea that we have husbands?"

"But you're both Missuses!" Rosie stumbled over the word.

"That's on account of our age and position. In service, all respectable single ladies of a certain age are Missus."

Rosie pondered, "What about Miss Payne, then?"

Cook sniffed. "That one doesn't admit to being over forty. Still thinks of herself as a girl. If you call her Missus, she won't answer." She lapsed into silence, then confided, "I nearly got married once, Rosie, years ago. But the young man I took a fancy to had no proper interest in food. Oh, he bolted it down all right, but he couldn't tell the difference between a tough piece of beef and the tasty morsel I'd cook. I couldn't spend my life with such a fellow, could I?"

"You could not." Rosie was definite.

"I've had plenty of offers since, but none I'd bother with, except perhaps Mr Harvey."

"Mr Harvey! Did he ask you?" Somehow, with his raised eyebrows, Mr Harvey seemed beyond marriage.

"He did. And partly I'd wish to. There is no one like Mr Harvey for appreciating good food. And he knows how to pay a compliment!" She lowered her voice confidentially. "He told me I was like one of my own apple pies, plump and flavoursome. Wasn't that beautiful?"

"If you say so, Mrs Biddle." Being compared to a fat apple tart was not Rosie's idea of romantic flattery.

There was no time to find out why Cook had turned the butler down.

Dinner had to be served at eight o'clock sharp to Lady de Courcy and Master Cyril in the small dining-room. Miss Florence had eaten earlier with Miss Payne in the nursery.

Although there were only three guests, Cook was in a tizzy. "Everything must be right," she told Rosie. "Her Ladyship doesn't usually entertain, not since the death of her dear husband. It's only because Lord Conville was a friend of his and is visiting the district with his wife and son, that she feels obliged to invite them. But I wish there were more guests, Rosie. And I want this to be a special occasion. There's no one like the gentry for appreciating proper cooking!

There was a constant to-ing and fro-ing from the kitchen by footmen with silver platters. They must be having about eight courses, thought Rosie, with different wines for every course.

A stuffed trout with a mournful expression gazed at her before it was whisked away to the dining-room. It was followed by game pie, then a sorbet to clear the palate. Roast beef and vegetables were next, then something called a syllabub. This was a dish of cream, curdled with orange liquer, flavoured with ginger and whisked to a froth. Cook let Rosie have a taste. It was food to die for!

But the meal was not yet over. After the syllabub came a golden moulded jelly in the shape of a castle, complete with drawbridge. Tiny pennants were stuck in the turrets and on its arrival in the dining-room, lavish compliments were immediately sent to Mrs Biddle. The cheese course was next. Rosie counted six different types. Finally, tea from Ceylon and coffee from Madagascar and a plate of Cook's iced biscuits completed the long meal.

There was a sudden flurry when a tall gentleman, dressed rather like the butler and puffing a large cigar, entered the kitchen. "Lord Conville!" someone whispered, awestruck. The maids curtsied and the footmen bowed and stood to attention. Close on his Lordship's heels was Mr Harvey.

"Lord Conville wishes to thank Mrs Biddle," the butler announced.

Cook was pushed forward, face steaming red from embarrassment and effort. Lord Conville gripped her hands in both of his, cigar clamped in his mouth.

"Magnificent repast! My dear Cook . . . magnificent!" Overwhelmed, he could say no more. Rosie thought she saw tears in his eyes. He patted Mrs Biddle's hand, clicked his heels, bowed and left the kitchen.

Rosie clapped and after staring at her for a moment, Mr Harvey enthusiastically followed suit. Soon everyone in the kitchen was applauding Cook and she had to sit down to recover.

Any envy Rosie might have felt towards the guests disappeared when at last the servants had their own dinner. Rosie counted seventeen at the huge table.

She was crammed into a corner between the upstairs and the downstairs maids. There were three housemaids, three footmen, a parlourmaid, Master Cyril's valet and a young man who told her he was "a thorough inside servant" with a perfect understanding of his business, which was "the care and maintenance of all plate, silver and furniture."

Joseph smiled and nodded at her. Jane, catching her eye, nearly had another fit of giggles. Mr Harvey presided at the top of the table with Mrs Smiley on one side and Mrs Biddle on the other.

The butler carved the meat and set a generous portion on each plate as it was handed to him. Then, in order of rank, each servant helped themselves to roast potatoes and vegetables.

Rosie knew at once why Lord Conville had been speechless. The meat almost melted in the mouth, it was so tender. And the gravy!

Mom had once made gravy from a packet which promptly went solid on the plate. It had looked like a turd. When Rosie had mentioned this, everyone's fork stopped mid-air and no one finished their dinner. Mom had been very unpleasant, but at least she hadn't attempted gravy again. Mrs Biddle's gravy was beautiful, tasting faintly of herbs and spices.

She was so busy eating and so tired, she paid little attention to the buzz of conversation, but it was a relief to know servants were allowed to talk. Dessert was a steaming apple pie. After one mouthful, Rosie understood Mr Harvey's compliment. Looking at the butler, she saw him smile at Mrs Biddle. A dark-haired man, he was quite distinguished looking, but very old, Rosie thought, at least forty-five. Too old to get married.

Rosie had only recently begun to see boys in a different light. They were still messers, but a lot of them were very nice looking, something she hadn't noticed before. Had Mr Harvey ever kissed Mrs Biddle? She stared at them. It wasn't possible.

What would it be like to kiss David Byrne? She liked his smile and the way – Rosie stopped. What was she thinking of? Exhaustion must be wrecking her head! Her eyes caught Joseph's and her face flamed, as if he'd read her thoughts. Then he smiled and she smiled back.

After the dishes and the tidying up, Rosie was at last ready for bed. She took a lighted candle – no oil lamps for the lesser servants – and staggered up to her room. She deposited the sconce on the table and groaned when she heard a knock on the door. "Oh no, not more work! Come in."

"Rosie. Mrs Biddle says I've to show you the po-pit and the laundry. You've to get your fresh apron and cap for tomorrow."

It was Jane. Rosie wondered how the girl could still smile after the long day.

"Don't you mind having to help me at this hour?"

"You'd do the same for me."

On their way, Jane chatted about the big house. "Mrs Smiley is a card, always acting cross, but very kindly. Now Cook is different, given to violent rages when things go wrong. She pushed one of the stable lads once into a load of horse manure. He was cheeky to her when she wore her new hat. Said it looked like a huge flower pot. Mr Harvey wanted to sack the boy immediately, but Cook would have none of it. She wouldn't hurt a flea really. Mr Harvey says she's an artist on account of her cooking and she has a delicate temperament."

Numb with tiredness, Rosie listened but said nothing. Jane looked at her. "I'm talking too much amn't I? Forgetting how tired you must be on your first day. And how strange you must find it all!"

She was so sympathetic Rosie thought for a moment of telling her exactly how strange everything was. But Gran had told her Jane did not believe in time travel. There was no point upsetting her.

In the laundry, Jane picked out the fresh clothing for the next day. Then she led Rosie out into a yard and down a lane. The moon bathed the trees in a silver light, their branches stretching towards the sky like skeletal arms.

"God, what a smell!" Rosie gasped.

"It's enough to make the dumb talk," Jane said. Rosie heard the amusement in her voice and smiled. She was good fun, her great, great gran.

They held their noses. "We deedn't go addy further todight." Jane told her. "The pit's ober there and idd's disgusting."

Ten minutes later, outside her bedroom Rosie paused. "You and your brother, do you get on well?"

"Joseph is the best person I know." Jane was fervent. "We have no other relatives and we look after each other. I don't know how I'd manage without him."

Rosie nodded. She watched as the girl went down the corridor, unaware of disaster ahead.

Thoughts of Jane's future troubled her and she now she was wide awake. Cyril was a powerful enemy, lord and master – almost – of this huge estate. It was easy for him to ruin the lives of two young servants.

Tossing and turning, Rosie did her best to sleep. She buried her head under the hard bolster and nearly suffocated. She counted all the books she'd read and recited her favourite American verse over and over:

Humpty Dumpty had a poor Summer
Humpty's Spring was an absolute bummer
Humpty's Winter was nothing at all
But Humpty Dumpty had a great Fall

It was no use. What was the point of trying to sleep when what she needed to do was to warn Joseph. If he knew what lay ahead then maybe, between them, they could do something about it.

Getting out of bed, she pulled on her dress and boots. In less than a minute she was knocking on Joseph's door.

Chapter 7

SHE STARED at the bleary-eyed boy. He was wearing a nightdress! Holding the candle closer, she realised it was actually a very long Grandad shirt. Rubbing his eyes, Joseph said, "You're Rosie. The new skivvy. The one that made a tremendous racket this morning. Is there anything wrong?"

Rosie shook her head. "I'm fine. But I'm worried about you."

The boy looked bewildered.

"Look. I've got to tell you something . . . "

He opened the door wider and she followed him into the room. Sitting on the edge of the bed, still holding the candle, he motioned her to a rickety chair.

Rosie told him about the conversation she'd overheard between the governess and Master Cyril. "They're out to get you!"

"Out where? Get me what? What do you mean?"

Rosie sighed. She kept forgetting that people in the past had a different way of saying things.

"They want you dismissed. Both of them are jealous because Lady de Courcy has taken a shine – likes you a lot. If I hadn't heard them they would've taken Florence's gold locket and blamed you. But they won't stop there. They intend to rob Lady de Courcy's diamond necklace and say you did it."

He looked disbelieving and she went on in a rush, "It's true. The police will come and you'll have to escape and you and Jane won't ever see each other again, probably."

He was not convinced. "I know Master Cyril doesn't like me, but he'd hardly go to so much trouble over the odd-job and gardener's boy. First a locket, now a diamond necklace! Perhaps you're a bit tired and imagining things."

"Have you ever travelled to the past, Joseph?"

The direct question drained the blood from his face. He could not speak and Rosie answered for him. "I know you have. I know it because I can time-travel too. We're related, Joseph."

He swallowed, looking at her intently as if he could read the truth of what she said in her eyes.

"Joseph, your sister is my great-great-grandmother."

Again he swallowed. Did he believe her? Was it too much for him to accept?

"You've come from the future then?" He was whispering.

"From the end of the next century. My grandmother said she heard you could journey through time. Only she didn't believe it. But I do. I have the same gift. That's how I came back here. That's why I know about the necklace."

The boy's eyes were wide as she told him the sparse details of Gran's story. Joseph sank down onto the edge of his bed, drinking in every word, staring at her all the time. When she'd finished Rosie realised he was more fascinated by her gift of time travel than by any news of impending disaster.

"What is it like, the future? Where you come from?"

Rosie tried to explain. She told him about electric lights and central heating and dishwashers because these were the things she missed most in Oak Park. He was most impressed, especially with switches. "Do you mean all you'd have to do is press something small and this room would light up? There are no candles? I'd give anything to see that!" He started staring at her again, still digesting all she had told him.

"Wait here," she said.

In a few minutes she was back with her store of food. She opened a can of coke and he recoiled from the hiss.

"Try it. It's a drink," she said.

Politely, raised the can to his lips. The liquid was cool and his eyes widened at the taste. He drank enthusiastically.

He had tasted chocolate before but not often and was delighted with the giant bars she gave him. He tried the fizz bags and the sharp taste of the powder made him catch his breath, but he finished the contents quickly, licking the last specks off his fingers. The popcorn did not appeal to him and he left it to one side, opening a packet of chocolate Kimberley. One bite and he was hooked. "Mmm, these are from heaven, Rosie." Within minutes he had eaten the whole lot. Burping with contentment, he said, "You come from wonderful times. I wish I could visit them. If you don't mind, I'll share the rest with Jane, though I won't tell her where you got them. She'd think our brains were addled."

Then for a moment he was quiet, his expression serious. "I thought I was the only time-traveller," he said. "I went back only once, three years ago . . ." He paused, the memories still painful.

Until now, Rosie hadn't quite believed someone else could have the same gift. She had thought herself isolated, that no one would understand. Now at last there was someone she could talk to and a weight lifted. Eagerly she plied the boy with questions. "Where did you go to? What year? Why?"

Joseph's voice was bleak. "I went back to find my grandfather, to a small village in Wexford. It was 1846." He glanced at Rosie who attached no importance to the date. "The Great Famine," he said. "Grandmother was dead and Mother was eleven years old. She and Grandfather were evicted because they could not pay the rent. They had no food, no way of surviving, so they had to go into different workhouses. She and Grandfather were separated, because they would not have males and females together. Mother never found out what had happened to him. She grieved over that." He stopped, old memories still raw.

"So you went back to find out?" Rosie was impatient.

"Mother said she'd never forget the day they were

separated. She could still see Grandfather's face." The boy was sombre. "So I went back." Again he stopped and Rosie began to be afraid.

"What happened, Joseph? Tell me. You did find him?"

"I found him and stayed with him. He was made to work in a quarry, breaking rock with a pickaxe and sledgehammer to make roads that went nowhere. It was called relief work. But there wasn't any relief in it. Not for Grandfather. He was not a strong man. When the weather was cold and wet he had no change of clothing. He got very ill. In a few weeks he was dead."

Rosie's heart dropped like a dead weight. Till this moment it had not occurred to her that the journey back might not bring a happy outcome. "So it was useless. You might as well not have gone."

"It was the best thing I ever did for Mother." He astonished her. "For I stayed with him until he was buried. One of his friends in the quarry was a stonemason and in secret he fashioned a gravestone with Grandfather's name and age on it. He was buried with a lot of other people and the grave would have been unmarked. But the stonemason helped me set the tombstone. When I got home, I was able to show Mother his grave. It gave her peace and she was happy to tend the spot."

"What became of your mother?"

"She was lucky. In the workhouse a woman who had lost her own child looked after her and made sure she got her share of food. When she was thirteen one of the female visitors offered her a position in her household. My father was groom there and when they married they got a cabin on the estate." Joseph grew quiet thinking of the past. Perhaps he didn't want to talk about it, Rosie thought, but then he said, "This is the first time I've spoken about her and Father since they died. Jane cries when I mention them, but I like to remember."

"Then what happened, Joseph?"

"Her time in the workhouse had a bad effect on Mother's health. She was always unwell. Then two years ago she caught a sickness, something in the lungs. She grew weaker and thinner and coughed for hours. The worst was when she coughed up so much blood, it formed a pool on the bedclothes. Father insisted on looking after her alone. He would not let us go near her, said we might catch her sickness as we were children and weaker than him. But it was he who caught the sickness and went down quickly, for he died the day after her."

For a while then, Joseph said nothing and Rosie did not disturb his thoughts. At last he raised his head and continued, "When they died the cabin was burned in case the sickness spread. There was no place for me and Jane on the estate. People were kind and sorry for us, but they thought we might spread the sickness and were glad when we left. We walked for days and were fortunate to find Oak Park."

"You were not lucky to find Cyril. He is jealous of you."

"He has no need," Joseph said. "He is rich and powerful and we are poor."

"There must be some reason for his jealousy. Gran said you made him look a fool twice, by being brave."

Joseph frowned, thinking. His brow cleared. "There was one occasion," he offered, "only one. Miss Florence's dog, Bunsy, fell into the river. She was playing with him while her brother and Lady de Courcy strolled along the bank. I was working in the gardens nearby and I heard Miss Florence screaming and the dog barking. When I got to the river Bunsy was struggling with the current. Miss Florence and Lady de Courcy were trying to rescue him with the branch of a tree, but the dog was being swept away. Master Cyril did not move. He stood like a statue on the bank while I raced past him, jumped in and got the dog out."

"Lady de Courcy was quite annoyed with him. He was the only one of the family who could swim, she said, and he had done nothing. I knew he hated to be spoken to in such a way, in front of a servant. To make matters worse, she praised me and gave me a guinea. Then she told him she there was to be no more talk of fit or unfit companions. I didn't understand this, but she said as far as she was concerned a person was as good as their deeds and I had proved my worth." Joseph looked at Rosie. "Does that explain why he might be jealous?"

"You made him look like the coward he is. That's why he hates you. And his mother was nice to you and mad with him."

"Oh, I don't think Lady de Courcy is at all mad," Joseph began earnestly.

Rosie sighed and cut him off. "I didn't mean she was mad," she said, "Well I did, but not insane mad, just annoyed mad. Ballistic. Ape. D'you see? Oh never mind. It doesn't matter."

Joseph would have argued the point, if he'd understood it. Was Rosie hinting that Lady de Courcy was a lunatic, or worse, some kind of wild monkey? It didn't make sense and he let it go.

Rosie changed the subject. "Have you Jane's cedarwood box?" He nodded.

"Give it back to her immediately. Tell her you'll fix it another time. If it's not in your room no one can plant the necklace in it."

"Plant? Like a flower?" Joseph frowned.

"We've got to change things." Rosie rushed on. "You'll have to avoid Cyril in case he sets you up – frames you – " Really, this was becoming impossible. "Gets you blamed for stealing the necklace." At last she managed to make him understand, but the effort was too much for her. "I have to go to bed," she said abruptly. "I'm too tired to speak any more."

At once Joseph was apologetic. "You must have some rest. We can talk more tomorrow. I can hardly believe I've found someone else who can travel through time."

Rosie was awakened by a crashing noise that swept in waves down the corridor and into the room, making her ears vibrate. Her heart thumping with fright, she jumped out of bed and ran to the door. There must be some disaster!

She saw the gleam of copper at the end of the corridor and a manservant swinging what looked like a sledgehammer against the surface of the gong. Everything shuddered.

"What on earth is wrong?" She ran down to him as soon as the last echo stopped wrecking her head. "Are we on fire? Are we being attacked?"

He gazed in astonishment at her rock star pyjamas, the faces of Blur and Oasis and the Cranberries eyeing him cheekily. Oh lord, she'd forgotten about them! She'd put them on after one look at the hideous nightdress that had been left under her pillow. There must have been at least fifty yards of material in it.

Why didn't the man answer her question?

"Are you deaf?" Rosie grew agitated. She did not want to burn to death waiting for a reply. "For heaven's sake, why are you banging that drum?" Seizing his arm, she shook him out of his astonishment.

"That gong is to wake you and the other servants."

"To wake us? To wake us! It'd wake the flamin' dead! Have you never heard of alarm clocks?"

"Indeed I have. The mistress has an alarm clock, but she is hardly likely to provide one for a skivvy, is she?"

Cheeky minx! Why was he having this conversation? And with someone dressed like a clown? Someone who'd roared at him. He'd show her!

Before Rosie could move, he struck the gong once more with all his force, then strolled away, leaving her to cope with the aftershock.

All morning her head vibrated. Cook and Mrs Smiley had her fetching and carrying for hours. So many orders: Bring butter from the dairy. Collect eggs. Fetch the milk – and don't forget those tin jugs. Ask the carpenter to fix the kitchen chair. Bring the carpet beater (Rosie thought it was an egg whisk) to the upstairs maid, whose apron she noticed was far more frilly than her own and who wore neat buttoned shoes under her grey dress. The maid smiled and looked friendly but there was no time for chat. Rosie had to fetch a barrel for pickling from the cooper and take towels to the laundry.

By mid-morning Rosie was beginning to realise just how big the estate was. It had its own dairy, carpenter's workshop and forge. She could not believe the amount of barrels in the cooperage. Here they made water barrels, tubs for washing clothes, churns for butter and, of course, barrels for pickling pork and bacon.

She passed the coach house on her way to the laundry and one of the men called her. "Like to have a look at her ladyship's coaches?" Rosie jumped at the offer. "They're not used half as much as they were in Lord de Courcy's time," he said wistfully. "Her ladyship don't accept so many invitations nowadays. But we like to keep them spanking!"

"I've never seen anything like them." Rosie's admiration was genuine and the coachman was delighted. He was not surprised at how little she knew and was pleased to give her a guided tour. "That small one is a dog cart. The children used it when they were younger to take them round the estate. Those plain ones are pony traps. Nice for a drive on a sunny day. Then there's the side car, for picking up guests from the station when it's not raining. That one there is the governess' cart. Miss Payne uses it on trips to the village. But this here is the pride of them all. This is the brougham."

Rosie was staring at a glossy dark blue coach, with a gold coat of arms, the like of which she'd only seen in old films about highwaymen, or royal processions on the telly. "It's a bit like the queen's coach," she said, "it's beautiful."

He laughed, basking in her praise. "Oh I expect Her Majesty's is more fancy. But we try to keep this one tip-top. It's only used for special occasions, for grand parties in Avondale and the like, but the family don't attend those so often now." He looked glum. "Her ladyship likes a quiet life these days."

Rosie traced the coat of arms lightly with her finger and said, "Can I see inside?"

His face lit up. "You can sit inside, pretend you're a lady. Why not?" He opened the carriage door, bowed and ushered her up the step. Rosie sat on the velvet seat and gazed at the blue watered-silk lining. "Those flaps beside you are for parcels," he told her. For a few moments she closed her eyes and pretended.

Before she left the coach house, he showed her his uniform for special occasions – dark blue livery, gold buttons, cockaded hat. Rosie was impressed and he was gratified. "If only her ladyship took as much interest," he sighed.

Delivering the towels to the laundry, Rosie was fascinated at the hive of activity. There were so many women working there. Watching closely, she saw that each washerwoman had three tubs; one for washing, one for rinsing and one for starching. They used washboards to scrub and mangles to squeeze out the water. There were long wooden rails for drying in bad weather. Next door, where Rosie went to fetch clean towels, clothes were ironed and crimped at a great rate. She learned that two of the stoves were used to heat up to seven irons at a time – and how different those irons looked. Flat irons for ordinary pressing, polishing irons to give a gloss to starched collars, crimping irons for ruffles and pleats. Then there were smoothing boards and sprinklers and drying frames shaped like hands, for gloves.

The washing machine and dryer at home were not things she usually thought about, and the steam iron was something she tried to avoid. Now she gave silent thanks that she did not have to go through all this labour to get her denims clean.

Her next task was to collect the vegetables for lunch. "They'll be in the storehouse by the gardens," Cook told her. "Ask young Joseph or Mr Smith the gardener to fill your basket with onions, turnips and carrots."

A small sign led to the vegetable plots and Rosie was surprised to find the place beautiful. She had entered a large garden, surrounded by ivy covered walls. Late roses and clematis climbed the trellised archways which flanked the gravel path. Between them were lines of apple and pear trees. Just beyond she found the vegetable plots and garden sheds.

Joseph was clearing an area for autumn sowing. He took her basket and filled it with Cook's orders while she waited on a bench nearby.

When he'd finished he sat beside her. "I shared out your food with Jane earlier. She cannot believe how beautiful it is. She especially liked that white lumpy stuff."

"The popcorn! I love it. Especially in the cinema."

Seeing his blank expression she told him all about cinemas and films. He was fascinated. "It's like magic!"

"Do you know what's been in my head all morning, Joseph?"

"I do. The sound of that gong. You told me at breakfast."

"Apart from that. I was thinking about us and how we can travel through time. I was wondering if you knew why we can do this? Why us? How did we get the power? And does it go back farther than you? From what Gran said, it's a gift passed down through our family, though she doesn't believe in it. Do you know anything at all about it, Joseph?"

The boy sat down beside her. "When I found Grandfather in the workhouse, he knew I was a time traveller from the way I spoke, what I did, what I knew about. He had been one himself, but lost the gift when he grew older. For many years he'd been waiting for someone like me. He regarded it as his duty to pass on what he knew to a believer and said I too would have to do so one day."

Rosie was agog. "I never knew it was a gift till Gran mentioned it. The first time, after I went back to 1956, I thought it might have been a dream. I'd been in an accident and had hurt my head so badly I was in a coma for a week. I wondered if my trip to the past wasn't my brain playing tricks on me. Then, when I went back to 1920, I knew it was no dream, but I still believed that blow to my head had something to do with it, that it had changed the way my mind worked. Then Gran mentioned you and I couldn't believe it. How did we get this gift? What did your grandfather tell you?"

"The older people in his family knew something about it, though none of them believed and none of them was able to time travel. He pieced their knowledge together and learned that his great-uncle, long dead, was the last person before him to possess the gift. It had come down to him through his great-grandmother. When she was a young girl some travelling players came to her village, acrobats, jugglers, such kind. One of the men was from the East, possibly India. The young girl married him.

To entertain the villagers he would send them into a trance and cause them to remember events they had no knowledge of in their everyday lives. The villagers thought it was some kind of trick, but he told his young wife these events belonged to previous lives.

"He believed that when we are born we hold in our minds and hearts the experiences of a long line of ancestors. Each life is a stepping stone on a lengthy journey and if we know how, we can step forwards or backwards in time. It is a matter of finding the stone and moving firmly onto it."

"And how do you do that?" Rosie asked, wanting her own thoughts confirmed.

Joseph explained, "You find a time and place of great turmoil in someone else's life. Someone connected to you, either in the past or in the future, who needs your help and whose energy reaches out and draws you into their life."

"But why us?" Rosie said. "And why not Gran? Or Mom? Or your sister Jane?"

"Because we believe in the gift and they don't. They cannot direct an energy, a force, they don't believe in. You must have a great desire to change the past and believe you can do so."

It made perfect sense, Rosie thought. It fitted in exactly

with her experience. Joseph had mentioned the future. The possibility fascinated her. Had he ever gone to the future?

He shook his head. "Grandfather said it was more difficult. He made such a journey once. We inherit something from the past, he said, but not from the future. To travel ahead drains so much energy that getting there and back can become the last journey. That was how he lost the gift. He told me he had great trouble returning to his own time and knew he had worn out his power."

"Where did he go?"

"I never found out. He was very tired and I left off questioning him. Then he got ill and it was too late."

"Perhaps he lost the gift because he stopped believing," Rosie said. "But wouldn't it be great to visit the future! Imagine a journey to the next century!"

She tried to visualise the world far beyond the year two thousand and could not. Joseph thought of the twentieth century and imagined faster transport, better machinery, more advanced weapons, but all vaguely. He could not foresee the scale of wars or the speed of travel. Televisions, computers, planes, astronauts were beyond the power of his imagination. He could not see the highways, the fighter jets, the hydrofoils and never dreamed of atom bombs or nuclear energy. But what little Rosie had told him whetted his appetite. And those chocolate biscuits were delicious. He longed to experience the future.

Lost in their reveries, neither heard Cook's scolding voice till she arrived in the garden. "Well I declare! Daydreaming in the sunshine while I have to collect the vegetables myself! You young folk are all the same, careless and flighty! Taking things lightly. Not doing things rightly. Sitting around, looking unsightly. Upsetting me mightily!"

Rosie was full of admiration. "That's very good," she said. "Did you just make up those rhymes?"

Mrs Biddle looked at her as if she were mad. Joseph got a fit of the giggles and hurriedly went back to his work.

Rosie followed the grumbling cook back to the house. "Master Cyril's looking for his lunch this hour. I had a mind to tell him to make it himself. Such a fusspot! Always in a black mood."

Reminded of Cyril, Rosie's spirits sank and her sense of adventure vanished.

Soon Cyril would make his move and if they weren't ready for him, Joseph's name would be disgraced and he and Jane would be separated forever.

Chapter 8

IN THE afternoon the weather changed. The day became heavy and overcast. The oil lamps were lit early and Cook grumbled with discomfort, "You can hardly breathe in this kitchen. The day is closing in. Mark my words, there'll be a thunderstorm soon."

Rosie was exhausted with the unaccustomed work and kept muttering to herself, "Five pounds a year. Pure slavery!" She wanted to sit down and rest. But Miss Payne had set her the task of beating the schoolroom rugs. She'd had to haul them down to the back line and whack them as hard as she could. A rug beater was different to a carpet beater in that it resembled a fly swat instead of an egg whisk. As soon as she walloped a rug a monstrous cloud of dust enveloped her. It was obvious they'd never been cleaned before and Rosie suspected Miss Payne was getting her revenge.

In ten minutes the air was thick and Rosie was bent double, coughing and spluttering. Still the dust billowed out. She was covered in grime and almost sobbing. When the skies opened and it began to rain, she could not believe her luck. She hauled the rugs from the line and staggered inside.

When Cook saw her filthy appearance and teary eyes, she took pity. "As soon as you've had a wash, Rosie, sit down here and try some of my fresh baking and home-made lemonade."

The delicious drink cleared her throat. It was made from

oranges and lemons. Rosie took a long glorious swallow and said, "Ah! That's even better than Coke."

"Coke? Coke!" Mrs Biddle could not believe it. Her face flushed dark red. "Are you saying my special recipe is like black coal?"

Rosie thought the poor woman would burst. "I am not," she said earnestly. "Your special recipe is the nicest drink I've ever had. Of course it's not like coal!"

Mollified, Cook sniffed. "Try these apple comfies," she said, placing some pastries on the table. Rosie took one bite and her eyes grew round. "Magic!" she breathed. They were as satisfying as gurcake, she thought, and Gran would love them. "Could I have the recipe?"

Mrs Biddle never revealed the secrets of her cooking and was about to refuse, when Rosie, wanting to repay her kindness, added, "Since it's too wet to beat those rugs, maybe I could read your brother's last letter for you and write a reply."

In her excitement, everything else went out of Cook's head and she rushed off. In no time she returned with the latest correspondence from Boston, plus paper, pen and ink.

"You've no idea how much this means to me, Rosie. It might seem silly to you, but I was too ashamed to ask anyone to read Michael's letters until you came along.

"I don't mind you because you're so young and I can boss you around and you look up to me, like . . . " She trailed off, reddening a little, then gathered herself together and said, "I'd best stop nattering and let you get on with it."

Rosie spread the letter on the table and read:

Main Street,
Boston
August 1870

Dearest Honoria Stacia,

I am sending this to Lady de Courcy's in the hope that you are still in employment at Oak Park, though it is hard to know, since you do not answer my letters. I know you have no book learning, but pray you will not be too proud to ask someone to read and write on your behalf, for I dearly long for news of you.

Boston has been a good place for me to settle after the war and my building trade has prospered. So many rich people want big houses (mansions they are called) on Constitution Hill and are prepared to pay a decent price. A man can make his fortune here if he is willing to work and by my reckoning, I shall soon be in a position to own such a house. Your brother will be one of the gentry!

My wife Etta and I would love for you to visit and if you say the word, we will send a ticket for your passage – more than one, if you have a husband and family. You can sail from Queenstown to New York where we will all meet you.

Our two boys and little girl are well and thriving. Next time I shall send a studio photograph and you will see how much little Honoria Stacia resembles you. She has the same frown and pretty much the same roar. But also like you, she is merry and big-hearted. Young Jack is like his mother, full of fun and Bernard takes after me. A tearaway, Etta calls him.

You must send us news, Sis. Etta is beginning to think I have no sister and am making you up. Every time I write she suggests maybe my old war wound is affecting my head. Since it was caused by a bullet in the shoulder, my brain is as good as ever. But I am beginning to wonder if some terrible fate has befallen you that you do not reply. So it would set both our minds at rest if we were to hear from you.

Your loving brother,
Michael

"Such a lot to take in," Cook breathed. "I didn't know he was married. And he wonders if I am wed. To think he's called his little girl after me." Her eyes misted.

Honoria Stacia, Rosie thought. Not a name she would have chosen herself. Quite a mouthful. "Why didn't you write back?" she said. "You could have asked Mr Harvey."

"I could not!" Cook was definite. "Mr Harvey doesn't know I cannot read. He is such a clever man, with a great respect for education. He would have no respect for me, if he knew I could neither read nor write."

"Is that why you won't marry him? Because he'd find out?"

Cook said nothing and Rosie knew she was right.

"But you are clever! This morning you knew exactly what was bought from the butcher over the last month and how much was was owing for each item. You had it all added up in your head. Most people would have to look through all the bills, but you did it without reading a word."

"Well I couldn't have done it *with* reading!" Cook was gruff. But Rosie's obvious sincerity flattered her. She hesitated a moment, then shyly asked, "Do you think you could help me to read, Rosie?"

Not in a few days, Rosie thought. "Mr Harvey would be much better than me at teaching you. He knows a lot more than I do. And he's always looking for ways to please you. He kept coming in this afternoon, asking could he help. 'Is there any way I could be of assistance, my dear Mrs Biddle?'" Rosie imitated the butler.

Cook blushed furiously. "Oh, I couldn't ask him. He'd think I was stupid!"

"He would not. He thinks you're wonderful. If you went mad and danced ballet on the table, he'd think you were wonderful!"

Cook blinked, then got a fit of laughing. "I could do the 'Dance of the Sugar Plum Fairy' that was in the Gaiety theatre last year." She choked, "I'd look lovely."

Rosie smiled at the image and pressed home her point. "Mr Harvey would love to help. And if you really liked him you'd ask him."

Mrs Biddle looked thoughtful. "Maybe I will then. But right now I must answer Michael. More than a year ago I ordered writing paper and pen and ink from Arnott's, always hoping I'd have occasion to use them."

Carefully Rosie dipped the nib of the wooden pen in the ink bottle and wrote a long letter on the thick creamy sheets of paper, giving all Mrs Biddle's news, making a special mention of Henry Harvey and ending with the hope that soon she would learn to read and write. Why these days, even the kitchen maids knew how.

When Rosie had finished, carefully drying the ink with the blotting paper and sealing the letter in the envelope, Mrs Biddle made her write down her recipe for apple comfies and home-made lemonade and extracted her promise never to reveal the ingredients.

Well, "never" couldn't mean 1997, Rosie thought.

Late in the evening the heavy atmosphere burst with a crash of thunder. The wind came whistling out of nowhere and lightning forked across the sky. Rain lashed down. Windows rattled. Doors slammed or flew open. Then for a few minutes there was a lull, while the elements gathered for a full-scale frenzy.

Round the servants' dinner table no one spoke as the earth groaned and the gale began to howl and shriek. A tremendous crash brought everyone to their feet.

"It's one of the oak trees!" Mr Harvey was galvanised into action. "Quickly, we must secure the house, close all the shutters. Mrs Biddle, perhaps you and young Rosie and Jane would bolt all the outer doors."

The girls followed Cook around the house, making the doors secure. On their way they saw the servants open the windows to grapple with the shutters and stagger from the force of the wind. Bits of debris came whirling inside the great house.

They had made their way back to the hall when Lady de Courcy appeared. "Cook, perhaps you could lend your assistance in the dining-room." Florence came racing down the stairs. "Mother, I heard a dreadful crash and then everything in the nursey toppled over. Miss Payne is putting it to rights. She wanted me to stay with her, but I had to know what happened!"

"A big oak tree fell," Rosie said.

Round-eyed, Florence followed them into the dining-room.

They could hardly believe their eyes. Cyril sat at the table ashen-faced, while dishes, cutlery, soup tureens, all vibrated. Overhead the chandeliers rocked, tipping their candles at such an angle that some fell to the floor. Flames were already licking the corner of the huge Persian carpet. Without asking permission, Jane tipped over what was left of the soup and doused the small blaze.

Rosie looked up, startled as the wall moaned. A stag's head eyed her and moved. She shrieked. The head shook and creaked, then crashed from the wall. She almost shrieked again when ornaments tumbled from the mantlepiece and smashed on the hearth. The wind whistled down through the chimney lifting the polar bear rug in front of the fire. The bared fangs grinned at her and Rosie shuddered.

"The servants have closed the shutters," Lady de Courcy had to shout to be heard. "But there is a gap and the wind is howling through the sashes." She was helpless. Cyril didn't move.

Cook took control. "Rosie, if any more candles fall, stamp on them immediately. Jane, take the dishes and cutlery from the table and stack them in that mahogany sideboard. Miss Florence, you can help too. Perhaps, Master Cyril, you'd like to assist?" Cyril did not budge. Lady de Courcy and Cook helped Florence clear the table. Jane packed everything into the sideboard.

Then Cook seized the linen tablecloth and dragged its weight across to the window. "I could do with your strength here Master Cyril, to push this cloth firmly between those sashes." She might as well have spoken to a statue. Sighing, Mrs Biddle hauled over one of the eighteenth century gilt dining-chairs and stood on it, practically ordering Lady de Courcy and Florence to feed up the heavy cloth while she jammed the sashes. The storm inside the room stopped. Rosie was having a great time hopping around the floor, stamping on candles. Cyril sat motionless as though there were no commotion.

Seeing his clenched hands, Rosie realised it was fear and not some kind of insane pride that kept him rigidly in place, while the rest of the household was in pandemonium.

Outside there was another sound, heartrending in its terror. Transfixed, they listened.

"It's the stables," Cook said. "The horses are maddened with fright."

Lady de Courcy put her hand on her son's shoulders. "Cyril, you cannot be the only one who sits idly by tonight." He said nothing, staring into the distance, hands still clenched.

Her voice rose. "You bring shame on this house, Cyril, and on your father's name. He would not have tolerated such cowardice."

Cyril bowed his head and all at once Rosie felt sorry for him. No one would choose to be so afraid. It wasn't his fault. Maybe something awful had happened him in the past. Glancing up, he caught her pitying look and stood abruptly. "You will see that I am no coward, Mother."

They followed him to the hall, where Mr Harvey and the manservants were already pouring out the main door, the quickest route to the stables. Joseph was with them.

Gripped with excitement, Rosie muttered to Jane and Florence, "Let's slip out with them." They needed no second bidding.

"This is an adventure!" Florence breathed. Once she stopped mid-race across the yard and did a dance of joy, holding up her face to the rain, unafraid of the wild storm. "This is much better than that old nursery and stuffy schoolroom!" She had to shout to be heard. Rosie gripped her arm and rushed her into the stables.

There Florence sobered up at once.

The horses were mad with terror, kicking at the stalls, rearing up, eyes rolling, mouths frothing. If they managed to batter their way free, they would cause havoc and injury and not only to themselves.

"Thank God you've brought help, Master Cyril," the head groom shouted through the din. "If we could have two more men in each stall, then there might be some hope of calming the horses. And you, Master Cyril, if you would take a taper to the lamps. Nearly all of them have gone out and we can barely see."

"My pony, Dingle, he's in the last stall!" Florence yelled.

"Let's get him out then." Jane rushed with her to the back of the stables.

Rosie stood in the shadows, longing to help, but not having a clue and knowing she'd do far more harm than good with the horses. They were very scary.

She saw Joseph approach a huge bay whose hind legs kicked out at the stall. He spoke softly, until at length the eyes stopped rolling, the ears pricked and the snorting and kicking ceased.

She saw Cyril take a taper and light it from one of the oil lamps. His hand was shaking. He made his way towards an unlit lamp. Suddenly, ahead of him, the stable door gusted open and lightning streaked across his path. Cyril shrieked and flinging the taper from him, rushed madly from the stables, knocking Rosie over in his desire to escape.

The taper had fallen near a heap of straw which quickly kindled and blazed. It was the horses who first noticed the smoke, with their keen sense of smell. The crackling flames added to their panic and once again they began their frantic battle for freedom. To Rosie it was a nightmare. The uproar of the horses and the desperate efforts of the men, the shadows, the dim lamps and the wild flashes of lightning, all combined to create a scene from hell. She was paralysed with terror.

Then, as if in slow motion, she saw Joseph move towards the fire, picking up a blanket on the way. She saw him beat the flames with the heavy cloth as they crackled around him, saw the servants come to his aid and the fire gradually smothered into submission. She saw Joseph become the centre of attention, heard him hailed as a hero and knew this was his second act of bravery and that Cyril would not be able to bear it.

Chapter 9

SHE WAS right. Cyril behaved in character.

He stumbled through the storm, back to the big house where his mother waited in the hall with Cook and Mrs Smiley. When the great door was closed with some difficulty behind him, he came towards them, dripping with rain and sweat.

"Where are the others? Are the horses safe?" Lady de Courcy asked.

He did not answer and her heart sank. "What happened, Cyril?" She shook him. "Tell me Cyril! What did you do?"

"You always seek to blame me, Mother." He was bitter.

"So tell me I am wrong then and nothing has happened."

He hesitated, still unable to look her in the eye, then, "It wasn't my fault. It was an accident. The taper started a fire. I could not think. The lightning . . . I had to get out . . ."

"There was a fire? You left the others in a burning stable?" Behind her she heard the two women gasp. Then both of them rushed forward. The great door would not budge. "The lock is strained," Mrs Smiley said. "Keep pulling!"

"You deserted them, Cyril! You ran away and left them to die!" Lady de Courcy was shaking him violently, while he twisted this way and that, eyes still on the ground.

"You coward! That a son of mine . . . I am glad your father is not alive to witness this."

Stung, Cyril wrenched himself from her grasp. "You forget,

Mother. One day I shall be master here. I am no servant, though you treat me like one. I am the future Lord de Courcy and should not have been ordered – expected – to do the work of stable boys. It is not my place to see to the horses!"

Furious, Lady de Courcy gripped his arm. But her reply was never made, for just then there was a hammering on the door. With an almighty push, the servants crowded in, the three girls at the front. At once Joseph was hoisted high onto the men's shoulders. They would not set him down till Mr Harvey had spoken.

"The horses are calmed My Lady. The grooms have them in charge and this lad was the hero of the hour. I never saw a braver deed!" Briefly he glanced at Cyril, his contempt barely masked.

Then he told how Joseph risked his life. "Surrounded by flames, my Lady, he took no thought for his life. Without him we should all be dead, horses and men." Again, he glanced at Cyril.

"It's true, Mother," Florence said. "He was very brave."

One of the servants stepped forward and shouted, "Three cheers for young Joseph!" Their shouts echoed through the hall. The housekeeper and cook joined in, and then Lady de Courcy.

The men set Joseph down and were silent as Lady de Courcy spoke. "No one could have better servants than I. You went far beyond the call of duty tonight to save property and animals which my son will inherit and from which you can never profit.

"Joseph, once again you have proved your courage and though I can never properly thank you, two gold sovereigns are yours. Your mother, were she alive, would be rightly proud of such a brave son.

"All of you have been diligent and courageous and have more than earned an extra five shillings. No woman has more loyal workers and you have all my gratitude and Cyril's."

Determined to make her son show his respect, she turned

towards him, but he was gone. He had slipped up the stairs when the men had surged forward and loudly cheered.

By the next day the storm had worn itself out and although the weather had not fully recovered, a pale sun was visible in the washed-out sky.

Cyril looked for Miss Payne early in the morning. This time there was no Rosie listening in the shadows.

Miss Payne had been on the landing when the servants had returned from the stables. She hadn't missed a thing. She was not impressed by Joseph. "Currying favour," she said. "His sister is just the same. A bad influence on Miss Florence who prefers her company to mine." She sniffed.

"Yes, yes." Cyril did not want to listen to these petty complaints. "When I am master you will have a position of honour in this household."

When he was master the irritating woman would have no place at all in Oak Park. Her sniffy disapproving face would be sent packing. In the meantime she was useful. He had lain awake all night, plotting Joseph's downfall and the plan he gave the governess was detailed. She had some questions.

"When shall we do it?"

"This afternoon when Mother takes her daily walk through her beloved gardens. At three o'clock I shall see Joseph, keep him occupied for half an hour. You will do the rest."

"What about that dratted skivvy? She admires the boy. What if she's around?"

Cyril smiled, "I have an errand for her – in the great maze." Miss Payne's eyebrows rose, then they both chuckled.

"Lord, what a trickster you are, Master Cyril. I well remember the last servant you sent to the maze. Lost for a full day, I think."

Cyril informed Cook that he wished to speak to Rosie after lunch.

"Why?" Cook was blunt. She knew the young master and did not want him upsetting the girl.

"Oh, Mother says it is time to take an interest in the household. I should get to know my servants, she says. Apparently, you are all human, much the same as us."

Cook ignored the veiled insult. "Why start with the skivvy?"

"I have to start somewhere, Mrs Biddle. The bottom seems as good a place as any. Send her into the drawing-room at two o'clock please."

"Master Cyril wants to see you," Cook told Rosie after lunch.

"What for?"

Cook shrugged, "Something daft, no doubt."

Mystified, Rosie went to the drawing-room where Cyril was already waiting. "I need you to run an errand for me, girl." He gazed at a spot above her head, then continued. "You may have noticed that it is my habit to read outdoors, while I am walking." Rosie had not, but she did not doubt him. Cyril continued, "This morning I was reading in the great maze and I left my book there. You must fetch it for me." His manner was imperious.

"What's the title?" Rosie's interest in books was aroused.

Cyril laughed, "It hardly matters to an ignorant peasant who cannot read or write. It's a book. It has pages and a cover."

"Is it a book of instructions?" Rosie said. Cyril rolled his eyes.

"I mean, does it tell you how to be such a pain in the neck?" She was furious. "Does it give lessons in insults? Or are you just naturally horrible?" She looked at him with mock pity. "You must've been born like that. Sad really. Maybe you could go to charm school."

Never in his life had Cyril been spoken to like this. No servant would have dared voice their dislike. He was caught between the desire to punch Rosie's mocking face and the need to get her out of the way. He could dismiss her, but then he would have to explain his actions to his mother and no doubt Cook would take the girl's side and complicate matters. Better to follow the plan.

"Just fetch my book!" he ordered. "You will find the maze beyond the west wing." He gestured vaguely and strode out of the room.

Rosie had never been in a maze and had she not been so excited at the prospect she might have wondered why Cyril did not react to her cheek. Out in the open, following his general directions, she found the small signpost and was soon standing in awe outside the maze. The hedge was dense and at least twice her own height. Eagerly she made for the entrance.

On the dot of three o'clock, when the servants had finished their lunch and were enjoying a little free time, Cyril knocked on Joseph's bedroom door. Having kept a close eye on his movements through Miss Payne, Cyril was not surprised to find him there.

Joseph eyed him warily. He had not yet returned Jane's box as Rosie advised and wondered was he now somehow going to regret this. But the older boy put on the act of his life. He smiled shyly at Joseph. "I wish to thank you for what you did last night."

Joseph was astounded. Cyril confided, "I'm afraid I panicked. God knows what would have happened if you hadn't fought that fire!"

"It was nothing."

"Oh but it was. For one thing it made quite an impression on Mother. She has rewarded you, now so must I."

"I didn't do it for any reward."

"Of course not. Nevertheless, the servants would think me most ungracious were you not to receive some token of my respect. Follow me please."

Joseph did as he was bid.

Outside Cyril's bedroom he stopped, unwilling to enter, until brusquely ordered to. Once inside he could not stop staring, fascinated and repelled at the same time. The bed took up only one corner of the huge room. The rest was set out like a natural history museum.

Large glass cases held stuffed grouse and pheasant, squirrels, a badger, two foxes, arranged in lifelike attitudes, glass eyes blank in death. On the walls, stags' heads gazed soulfully while underneath them, on two long tables, were glass trays of dead butterflies.

"What do you think?" For once Cyril's eagerness wasn't feigned.

"Very . . . interesting."

Cyril's room faced north and got little sunlight. The shadows and the dead creatures created an eerie atmosphere. To Joseph it was a chamber of horrors.

"You know, I prepared these animals myself," Cyril went on. "When Father was alive, he allowed me study taxidermy with a Dublin specialist who does all the work for the Charleville estate."

His enthusiasm grew. "At last year's December shoot there, seven thousand creatures were killed. All species, including pheasant, hare, woodcock, ferret, snipe and grouse. Was that not magnificent? The display was excellent, using animals which had been snared and not ruined by shot. A marvel!"

Remembering the stories he'd heard of poachers jailed for killing a few rabbits, Joseph could not be so enthusiastic. Seeing his grim expression, Cyril's face went dark.

"Well . . . what would you know of such things? You are no aristocrat. Come, look at these." He showed the boy row upon row of pinned exotic butterflies. Their vivid colours belonged to life, not death. Joseph imagined them dancing in the sunlight, innocent and free.

"I wish to give you one of these trays, Joseph, as my reward."

When the boy didn't answer, wouldn't even look at him, his eyes narrowed. "You should be grateful. They are, all of them, magnificent specimens, caught in India, Africa and the hot Mediterranean countries."

"They are beautiful," Joseph said and Cyril was appeased till he went on, "but what good are they dead? What good are they in this room for only you to look at?"

"Do you want a tray or not?" Cyril would have liked to order the wretch out. He consulted his pocket watch. Still five minutes to go.

Joseph did not want to annoy the young master further. He stared at the trays for some time, wondering why Cyril kept taking out his watch.

"I'll take those." The boy pointed to a section of butterflies with wings as golden as the sun. There was no gratitude in his voice and once again Cyril was tempted to exercise some power. Time enough for that. Instead he held his temper, looked at his watch once more and smiled. "Take it then." Joseph lifted the tray and left the room without another word.

Chapter 10

LATER, CYRIL waited in the small sittingroom for his mother to seek him out, when she had made her discovery. For once he was feeling quite happy. He had made a plan – quite a good plan – and so far it was working out. His father used to speak of strategy. "The best military leaders plan carefully," he used to say. "They foresee difficulties long before they happen and avoid them."

His father, who had once been a colonel in the Indian army, would have been proud of him today, Cyril thought. He had taken the initiative for once, not waited on his mother's orders. He was pleased with himself.

While he waited, his eyes scanned *The Irish Times*. Idly he noted the lists of distinguished visitors at the Dublin hotels:

"The youthful Mr Parnell of Avondale, will be staying at the Gresham Hotel for the next three days."

"The Shelbourne extends a welcome to the following distinguished guests: Lady Astor, Mr William Morriss of London and Mr John Yeats, the renowned artist. Their presence graces this establishment for the next week."

The advertisements were endless – for Sunday train excursions to Arklow, positions for servants, illustrated clothes for fashion shops. There were some dispatches from the Franco Prussian war, but Cyril barely glanced at them. He was becoming impatient. Where on earth was his mother?

Upstairs a door slammed, then he heard Lady de Courcy's

hurrying footsteps on the marble staircase and the rustle of silk as she drew nearer. He smiled and pretended to be engrossed in the paper.

"Cyril! Cyril!" She was almost hysterical. He appeared to drag himself away from the news.

Distraught, his mother took some moments to tell him what was wrong. "The necklace, Cyril. The diamond necklace. The one your dear father gave me on our first wedding anniversary. It's gone from my dressing table."

"The diamonds of Kashmir?" Cyril pretended shock and horror.

"What on earth does Kashmir matter?" Lady de Courcy cried. Really, sometimes her son was an imbecile. "The necklace is precious to me because it was your father's gift. Now it has disappeared!"

"Are you sure, Mother?"

"Cyril, you are an idiot." Lady de Courcy was too upset to be tactful. "You know my routine. Every afternoon I like to look at that necklace and remember your father. Every afternoon I leave it on my dressing table in the velvet pouch. It is my habit. Then I go for my walk and look forward to remembering old times. Always when I come back, I set out the diamonds. Sometimes I read his letters again. It is my way of finding comfort, Cyril. You know that. Now the necklace is gone!"

Cyril rose to his feet. "Well, of course, you are far too familiar with the servants, Mother. No doubt one of them has taken advantage." He made for the door. "I shall ask Mr Harvey to summon everyone who has been in the house since lunchtime."

He strode from the room and within half an hour, the servants were gathered in the hall. Lady de Courcy and Florence stood at the bottom of the staircase, while Cyril was half way up, ready to address the assembly.

It had taken Mr Harvey some time to locate Joseph and Rosie. The boy had been found near one of the great oak trees, gently lifting the glass from a tray of butterflies, detaching their pins and setting them out on a fine crock-of-gold shawl. The servant who had found him got short shrift when he asked for an explanation. "He said the butterflies were his, Mr Harvey. Master Cyril gave them to him. And it was his Mother's shawl. He was burying the butterflies under one of the oak trees so they would lie among the golden spring daffodils. I reckon he's gone off his head, Mr Harvey, shock from the fire maybe. So I let him be. He said he would be in quickly after me."

Another servant had trotted everywhere, looking for Rosie. Master Cyril said he hadn't seen her since two o' clock and what was the point of looking for her. She wasn't important. But Cook was insistent and the servant loved his food, so he went willingly. Luckily, one of the laundry maids had seen her go in the direction of the maze. When he got there he could hear the girl calling, "Help! Help! Get me out!"

Helplessness turned to rage. "That fool, Cyril! I'll punch his face in. Help!"

The voice grew plaintive, "Please, please, someone help!"

The servant recognised despair. He knew his way around the maze and had soon rescued her.

If Cyril was surprised to see her he did not show it.

Curtly, he told his respectful audience that one of them had stolen Lady de Courcy's necklace. He ignored his mother's protests. She had hoped he would seek the co-operation of the servants, not blame them outright and without proof. Upset by the loss of her husband's gift, she was unable to cope with her son.

"Of course one of these people took it!" Cyril insisted, "Who else could it have been?"

The servants were silent. Rosie was dismayed. She saw a look pass between Cyril and Miss Payne, who coughed and said, "I feel it is my duty to speak up. I saw the necklace this afternoon."

Joseph's face was tense and Rosie groaned. They both knew what was coming next and it was too late to stop it. Miss Payne paused for effect, unable to hide a slight smile before she continued, "It *was* one of the servants who took the necklace, one of the lowest orders, needless to say, someone whose head has been turned by too much praise in recent days – " Catching Cyril's frown she hurried on, raising her voice and pointing dramatically at Joseph. "It was that boy, of whom you all think a great deal. But I tell you now, he is a common thief."

Rosie had to admire her acting. She was very convincing, her anger sounded real. That's because it is real, the girl thought. She hates Joseph and wishes so hard this were all true.

Miss Payne was standing in front of him now, practically shrieking. "I saw him come out of Lady de Courcy's room before half past three. The necklace was in his hands, spilling out of its velvet pouch."

Joseph raised a hand in protest and Miss Payne cowered. "See! He will strike me as he threatened. He warned me to say nothing or I would be harmed. I was terrified and could not think what to do. But I know my duty. *He* is the thief!"

There was a murmur of disagreement. Then Joseph stepped forward. "I was in Master Cyril's room at the time Miss Payne says she saw me. He knows the truth."

Cyril smiled grimly. "You may well have been in my room, but not at my invitation. I was in the Oak arbour until an hour ago."

"But you gave me a tray of butterflies!"

Cyril was scornful. "Why should I do that? Everyone knows my feelings as far as you are concerned. I am not likely to give you anything." He paused. Some of the servants looked puzzled. It was true what the master said. Doubts began to set in.

"You are lying," Cyril went on, "trying to fool people just as you have fooled my mother, tricked her and now robbed her. Why would I give you anything?"

Rosie closed her eyes. Really, Cyril was very clever.

Miss Payne added insult to injury. "So that's what it was! He was carrying something large hidden under a cloth. He could not manage it and hold the necklace properly at the same time. That's why the jewels were falling out of the pouch."

Cyril did not bother to hide his triumph. "You stole those butterflies. Why don't you admit it? No one believes I gave them to you. What have you done with them?"

Joseph's voice was steady. "I stole nothing. Not the necklace, not the butterflies. You made me a gift this afternoon, to do with it what I wanted. I buried the butterflies."

Victory changed to fury and Cyril raged, "You buried them! You clot. You stupid, stupid *slave*! They are a rare species, worth a fortune. Tell me at once where you buried them!"

The boy did not answer and the servant who had seen the burial said nothing. Master Cyril had no business calling anyone a slave.

Lady de Courcy took matters into her own hands. "You have been a good servant, Joseph, risking your life twice on our behalf. I find it hard to believe you would steal from me."

The gathering muttered in agreement, "That's true. He wouldn't do that. It doesn't make sense."

Cyril tried to intervene, but his mother waved a hand and told him fiecely to let the boy talk.

"I wouldn't steal. I didn't. You can search my room. I've nothing to hide."

Immediately Cyril dispatched Mr Harvey and a footman. In silence everyone waited. Some time later the two returned, relieved and smiling.

"Nothing my Lady. We searched the room, every possible hiding place. Nothing."

Cyril was stunned. He shot Miss Payne a venomous look, but she looked just as shocked.

Recovering, he said, "Mother, a cunning thief would not

have hidden such a fortune in his room. He had time to put the necklace elsewhere. There is no doubt about his guilt. After all, Miss Payne saw him and he has admitted to the butterflies. Perhaps he buried the diamonds with them."

"Joseph has denied stealing anything!" Lady de Courcy said sharply. "Either you are not listening, Cyril, or you want very badly for him to be guilty."

And Florence, who had said nothing till now, piped up, "Joseph isn't a thief. You hate him, Cyril, and that's why you're doing this! You hate him because he is my friend and because Mother likes him."

She could say no more, her face white with strain.

Lady de Courcy put a comforting hand on her shoulder and in the hall there was an embarrassed shuffling.

"I'll show you where the butterflies are," Joseph sighed. "There's no necklace with them."

Again Mr Harvey and the footman left, this time accompanied by the boy and Cyril.

When they returned, Cyril was spluttering with rage, holding a small heap of muddy objects in the now soiled shawl. He pointed accusingly at the footman. "That idiot took no care in his digging and hacked the precious specimens to pieces.Then he emptied this stupid piece of cloth into the clay and destroyed what was left."

His mother had no sympathy. "You should have used the spade yourself. Did you find the diamonds?" Angrily he shook his head and tried to figure out what had gone wrong. His eyes glittered as he noticed Rosie staring coolly at him. There was something about her – something knowing – that he did not like. Perhaps he should have her searched. But there was no point. She had been out of the way all afternoon. It wasn't possible she knew about his plan, never mind managed to foil it.

Lady de Courcy came to a decision, "I will make no judgements yet. It would surprise me greatly if Joseph were the guilty party. Nevertheless, we must take into account what Miss Payne thinks she saw, yet I cannot believe young Joseph is such a villain. There must be some misunderstanding over the butterflies. Hush now Cyril!" About to say something, her son changed his mind.

Lady de Courcy put a hand to her forehead. "My sister Mabel is expecting my arrival in Merrion Square tomorow. Everything is almost packed. I shall bring forward my plans and we will go within the hour. Not you, Cyril. You take charge here. Florence will accompany me, and the maid, Jane. I shall give these matters serious thought and will deal with them on Sunday when I return. In the meantime, Mr Harvey can arrange a general search of the estate."

Wearily she dismissed the assembly and made her way up the stairs. The servants crowded around Joseph offering sympathy.

Jane took Rosie's arm. "If you can, will you help my brother while I'm away?"

Rosie nodded and the girl went on, "I know it's a strange thing to ask, seeing as we hardly know you, but I feel you are our friend. You gave us that lovely food. Joseph made me promise not to ask about it. There's something about you . . . something familiar, but we never met before two days ago, did we?"

Rosie shook her head and Jane sighed. "I'm just being foolish, imagining things. Please give Joseph your help. I'd best say goodbye to him and get ready for Dublin."

After a few words with her brother Jane was gone. The rest of the servants drifted away and Rosie tackled Joseph.

"What did you do with Jane's cedarwood box?" she asked.

"I put it back. After Master Cyril gave me the butterflies I took them to my room, to decide what to do with them. I saw the box and remembered what you'd said, so I returned it before burying the butterflies."

Exasperated, Rosie said, "Didn't you notice anything rattling? Like a necklace?"

Joseph drew in his breath. "There was no rattle. But then it was probably in a pouch. Now that I think of it, the box did seem heavier, but I was in a hurry, late for my duties and I wanted to look after the butterflies. I did not stop to think."

Rosie felt like tearing out her hair, or better still, his. "But I *warned* you." She wailed. "I told you they'd put the necklace in the box!"

"You told me not to go near Lady de Courcy's room. I thought I was safe unless somehow they tried to trick me into going there."

"Where's Jane now?"

"I expect she's helping Miss Florence to pack."

"Right. I'm off to get the necklace!"

Racing up the backstairs, Rosie hurtled down the dark corridor and into Jane's room. She saw the cedarwood box on the washstand. In seconds the necklace was deep in the pocket of her dress and she was running back down.

Gasping, she barely had time to nod breathlessly at Joseph before Mrs Smiley came into the hall. "I've been looking for you two and thank goodness I don't have to climb all those stairs again to find you. There's several tasks need doing – what's wrong with your breathing, young Rosie?"

Rosie spluttered and heaved. "I'm all right," she wheezed.

"I think she swallowed something." Joseph was trying to be helpful.

"Oh, and you're just standin' there while she chokes to death!" Galvanised into action, Mrs Smiley gave Rosie such a whack on the back the girl went staggering across the hall. As the housekeeper strode purposefully towards her, Rosie raised a hand. "Don't touch me," she managed, gasping. "I think my back is broken."

Moving away from the large woman she gulped in the air until her breathing was normal. Why on earth did people think great wallops between the shoulder blades helped anyone to breathe?

Satisfied that Rosie was once more in the full of her health, Mrs Smiley gave them their orders and sent them on their way.

By the time their work was finished, Lady de Courcy had left for Dublin with Florence and Jane.

Chapter 11

EARLY NEXT morning Cyril summoned the servants once more to the hall.

"Not again," Cook grumbled. "He'll drive us all mad."

"That won't bother him," Mrs Smiley said. "He takes delight in torturing others."

Mr Harvey was disapproving, "Now, now. We must have some respect."

The housekeeper grunted and left the kitchen. Only Cook and the butler remained.

"Mr Harvey, do you think that necklace was robbed? Do you think Joseph will be blamed?"

"You are a sensitive lady, Mrs Biddle, to worry so," said the butler. "I think perhaps the necklace has been mislaid. Master Cyril can't see straight. His dislike of young Joseph does him no credit. Why would the boy risk his life for her ladyship's horses one day and rob her jewels the next? The necklace will turn up, don't you worry, and Lady de Courcy will sort out this sorry affair."

"That's what I hope too," Mrs Biddle said, then gathered her courage, "Mr Harvey, I would like your help."

Mr Harvey pushed back his chair and rose, overcome. "My dear Mrs Biddle. You only have to ask. You are welcome to far more than whatever miserable help I could give a woman of your stature."

Taken aback, Mrs Biddle said, "Are you referring to my size, Mr Harvey? I cannot help being a large woman."

"Mrs Biddle, your size is perfect. Perfect! You are a splendid woman. I was referring to your respected position in the household. Only ask, Mrs Biddle, and you are assured of my assistance."

Cook took a deep breath. "I can't read, Mr Harvey. There, now I've said it. No doubt you'll think I'm stupid and I daresay I am and won't blame you if you have nothing more to do with me." Her face was brick red and it took her some time to look the butler in the eye.

He was beaming, somewhat foolishly. Was he laughing at her, she wondered. Did he think she was some kind of joke? Her face went even redder and she frowned, but before she could say anything Mr Harvey gripped her hand and said, "My dear lady, how could you ever have had time to learn to read and write? What with all the knowledge you've had to acquire about cooking – and such superior cuisine at that! – Not to mention kitchen management, staff supervision, trading with shopkeepers and dealing with the aristocracy. You are a woman of so many talents, Mrs Biddle."

Cook's face would have gone even redder with pleasure if that were possible.

The butler seized his advantage, "Of course I shall teach you to read and write. But it would be so much easier if you were to marry me. For then we could have our own place, a small house on the estate perhaps, and we could have privacy, no prying eyes to embarrass you."

Cook said nothing, overcome.

Afraid he had gone too far and she would never speak to him again, Mr Harvey rushed on, "Not that I am suggesting you should be in any way ashamed, Mrs Biddle! You would make me a proud man if you accepted my offer. I have asked you before and perhaps I am too forward, thinking you might have changed your mind. But it would be an honour . . ."

He waited and was rewarded with a big smile. "What a good idea, Mr Harvey. Certainly we should marry." They beamed at each other, Mr Harvey squeezing both her hands, hurriedly letting go when Rosie stuck her head in the door.

"Cyril says he wants you two out in the hall now. He says you're to put some manners on the servants, Mr Harvey, and make them listen. Really, he should try a few manners himself some time. He's the rudest person I ever met . . . well, except for Miss Hackett in 1956." The head disappeared again.

"Such an extraordinary girl." Mr Harvey's voice was faint. "Does she know she's a scullery maid and not meant to have any opinions, never mind express them? I fear she won't last long."

"Oh yes she will!" said Cook fiercely. "But I wonder who Miss Hackett is. Not pleasant by all accounts. She must have meant 1856, though she wasn't even born then."

"Perhaps she's astray in the head, a young lunatic," Mr Harvey said. Then catching Cook's glare, he amended hastily, "Well, perhaps not, though she does seem a little strange. Or would 'different' be a better word? My dear Mrs Biddle, we'd best go and hear what Master Cyril has to say."

And Mrs Biddle, who thought first names were now in order, but was acutely embarassed, said in a very low voice, "Do call me Honoria Stacia."

"Glorious spacious what, my dear?" Mr Harvey had misheard.

Cook went red and was raging with herself for being so awkward. "It's my name!" She was shouting, not wanting any more mistakes.

The butler was bewildered. "Your name? Glorious Spacious is your name?"

"*Honoria Stacia!*" Cook yelled. She was nearly purple.

"Oh. Oh, I see. What a graceful, dignified name. So perfect, my dear. I wouldn't have expected anything less. Mine is rather simpler, I'm afraid. Plain Henry."

"Henry Harvey," Cook breathed. "Very nice."

They smiled at each other. Then the butler opened the door for Mrs Biddle, gave a ceremonious bow and ushered her out of the kitchen.

For a moment Mr Harvey thought the hall was full of

maniacs. Servants were shouting and jostling, trying to be heard, while Cyril was almost cowering at the foot of the stairs.

The butler took control at once. He climbed one quarter of the way up the marble staircase, then when he had a good view, he stared at the mob below until one by one they quietened and there was silence.

"Hannigan!" He addressed the tall footman. "Explain matters."

Hannigan was indignant, "Master Cyril's only gone and called the Constabulary to arrest young Joseph here!"

There was an outbreak of indignation again, some of the servants even raising their fists. Mr Harvey lifted a hand and again there was silence.

"Is this true, Master Cyril? In spite of your mother's wishes, you have done this?"

Cyril swallowed and moved up the stairs until he was on the step above the butler, protected by his bulk.

"Lady de Courcy left me in charge," he said. "If any of you object then you may leave at once and with no good word."

There was a groan. Without a reference, none of them could hope for another position. Cyril continued, "Yes, I have called the constabulary. The servant I sent returned with the message that they cannot come until tomorrow." His smile was malicious now. "One of Lord Mowbrey's tenants refused to pay extra rent and will not leave his cottage. He and his family must be forcibly removed today and the police are required to help at the eviction."

Astonished, Mr Harvey turned to him. "But what about the Land Acts? The law promises fair rents for tenants and no evictions once they are paid."

"Does it indeed?" sneered Cyril, "Well, you'll find the Land Acts won't work in Wicklow. The constabulary will see to that! The landlord must do his duty when the tenant won't pay!"

Voices rose in anger:

"Rackrents! How could anyone meet Mowbrey's demands?"

"Throwing families onto the roadsides. Shame!"

"The landlords want our blood!"

"If they do, we'll spill some of theirs first!"

There was a surge towards the staircase. However, when Mr Harvey took a step down, the noise ceased.

Cyril moved up a few steps and shouted, "I shall not tolerate Fenians on my estate! You would be well advised to remember what happened in '67. The Fenians were badly beaten then. Only three years ago! They have no hope now. And if any here have sympathy with those who break the law and don't pay their due rent, let them leave now. *I will not have them in my house!*"

Incensed, the servants clenched their fists, then one of them called, "It's not your house. Your good mother is not dead yet. She would never evict a poor family. A cheer for Lady de Courcy!"

Cyril could not see the speaker and anyway he could hardly object to a cheer for his mother from the servants. But as the shouts rose to the rafters, he fumed with rage and when silence returned, he announced coldly, "I summoned you to let you know the constabulary will arrive sometime tomorrow to arrest that common thief, Joseph O'Neill. Now you may return to your duties."

They looked at Mr Harvey, refusing to obey Cyril.

"We'd best do as he says," the butler told them and silently they filed away, Rosie following Joseph.

Tugging at his sleeve she murmured, "We'd better talk," and they slipped out the back door into the yard. Rosie did not waste time. "Lady de Courcy won't be home until Sunday. If we put the necklace back now, Cyril will still do everything he can to hurt you. Even if the police find the necklace and you're in the clear, Cyril will try to get rid of you before his mother comes home."

"What if I left now? There's an old empty cottage on the estate. I can stay there until her ladyship comes back."

"Cyril will search everywhere. He knows his mother likes you and doesn't want to believe you could do anything bad. He'll find you and think up some other way to get rid of you. And he'll make sure your sister leaves too. You won't see Jane ever again." Joseph grew agitated, "There is nothing I can do then? We're finished."

But Rosie was devising a plan.

"We could go home," she mused, thinking aloud. "Back to my time for a few days. Cyril will never find you there. He'll look everywhere on the estate, but then he'll think you've run away. We can come back, sneak in and return the necklace just before Lady de Courcy comes home. She'll find it and everyone will think it's all been a big mistake – except for sneaky Cyril and pasty-faced Payne! And with his mother home, he won't be able to do a thing. What do you think?"

She was not prepared for Joseph's enthusiasm. He gripped her arm, "A stroke of genius," he said. His eyes were alight at the prospect. Although it was her plan, Rosie felt obliged to warn him, "You've never travelled to the future. It could be a terrifying experience." She thought of the traffic, the noise, the flashing neon lights of the city. Such a contrast to this quiet country existence.

He was still gripping her arm in excitement. "It will be the adventure of a lifetime! And I'll have you with me to explain everything. Why would I be terrified?"

She felt it only fair to point out, "You may lose your gift, Joseph. You may never travel again. Remember what your grandfather told you."

"Rosie, I must go. The chance will never come again. Besides, I'd rather lose the gift than lose my sister. She is the only family I have and I must look after her. What would she do without me? It's a marvellous idea!"

It was the only way to keep him safe from Cyril, Rosie thought. She told him her plan.

"The Dublin bus comes at eleven. No, I don't have time to explain what a bus is. A bit like a carriage without horses. We have to be in 1997 just as it's arriving. That way there's less risk of my teachers or class seeing us. So, in exactly one hour's time, meet me at the end of the front avenue, outside the gates and down a bit from the lodge."

Rosie sped up to her room, aware that Cook and Mrs Smiley or even Miss Payne must be looking for her.

What would she need? No point in taking the rucksack. She would hide it in Jane's room, safe from curious eyes. No one would see her tape recorder or twentieth century clothes. She'd best leave her anorak behind too. She couldn't wear it leaving the house. It would only draw attention. House keys and money, that was all she had to bring. And of course the necklace. Nobody here must find it before the time came to put it back.

With ten minutes to spare, she was outside the front gate, out of sight of the family living in the gate lodge, pacing up and down, frozen because she had no coat.

If Joseph did not arrive quickly, she would have to go without him. Where on earth was he? Then she saw him clattering towards her, jacket swinging over his striped apron.

"Mr Harvey was talking to me for an age," the boy said breathlessly. "He didn't want me to worry about the polis. I was nearly doing a jig, wanting him to go, but that made him worse. He kept saying I was very agitated. And the police might take that for guilt and I must remain calm."

"How did you get rid of him?"

"I didn't. I just ran away from him."

"Oh well," Rosie said. "He'll put it down to nerves."

She pulled him across the road to the stone wall.

"We'd best hold hands so we don't lose each other." Joseph was anxious.

"Hang on till I fix my watch."

"I've never seen one like that before," Joseph was agog. "It's very strange."

"It is not. It's beautiful. It has all the time zones and a light and the date and you can use it as a stop watch! But you haven't time to look at it now. We've got to concentrate."

She gripped his hand. "Think October 1997."

But there was no change in the still Autumn day, the silence broken only by birdsong and rustling leaves. Eyes closed, faces solemn, hands clasped, they stood on the empty country road and nothing happened. Time was running out.

Rosie opened her eyes. "It won't work." She was desperate. "I can't get back!"

She would never see her family or friends again! "I'm stranded!" Panicking, she could not focus on the task in hand, overcome by grief and a huge sense of loss.

"You're not stranded, Rosie. Do you have the necklace?"

Rosie blinked. What was he on about?

"The necklace, Rosie! It could help us. After all, it's one reason you came back. If your grandmother hadn't told you about it, you wouldn't be here, trying to change things. It's the link between my time and yours. Please, Rosie! Where is it?"

She dug deep in her pocket. Then, opening her fist, she showed him the velvet pouch and he placed his hand on it. Together they wished: "October 1997."

Then there was a kind of tremor, a rumbling from the ground. For a moment the birds stopped singing and the trees rustled more vigorously as a sudden wind swept through them. The air changed, the scent of hawthorn overlaid with something far less pleasant. Bus fumes. She opened her eyes and saw the single decker turn the corner towards them.

"Joseph, we've done it!"

But he would not look and seeing his pale tense face, she realised that for all his brave talk, he was scared.

"*Joseph!* The bus is here!"

He was still clutching her hand and would not let go, his eyes squeezed tight. With her free hand she punched his arm.

"Ouch!" Involuntarily he opened his eyes and nearly fainted when he saw the approaching bus, coughing and spluttering its way towards them. He backed into the wall as the airbrakes hissed and the gears grated.

"It's a monster," he whispered.

"It's a bus," Rosie said. "Think of trains. Well, this is like a very short train, only it doesn't run on tracks. Come on, we've got to get on."

She dragged him over. He had almost found his courage when the doors hissed at him and folded abruptly back. He would have pulled away then, but she would not let go and hauled him up after her, holding onto him with one hand while she rooted for money with the other in her apron pocket.

Joseph was staring at the dials in front of the driver. The driver was just as astonished.

"What sort of a get-up are the two of you wearing? It's a bit early in the season for pantos."

Rosie glared at him and he lowered his voice, nodding in Joseph's direction. "Is your man a bit simple? You don't find too many fellas his age wearing an apron. He's like something out of Dickens in those trousers. And you'd think he'd never seen a bus the way he was skitterin' all over the road. 'Course you don't look the full shilling yourself either . . . "

Appalled, Rosie realised their clothes had not changed. Joseph was in his plus-fours and high-collared shirt. They were both wearing aprons and she had on the hideous grey maid's dress with the starched white collar.

The driver kept looking at boy, who was staring at everything with a stunned expression.

"He is a bit simple isn't he? He looks as if he's on another planet."

"Are you going to give us our tickets? And it's not good manners to comment on people's appearance!" Mom had once said this when Rosie had pointed at a man in O'Connell Street, who was wearing a plastic bag on his head. At the time she hadn't agreed and wanted to ask the man about his strange headgear, but now she found the phrase useful.

Taken aback, the driver issued two tickets. Then he winked. "Your hat is beautiful, love. I'd fancy one for myself."

Scarlet, Rosie pulled Joseph along the bus, sat down near the back and yanked off the maid's cap, glaring all the time at the passengers who were craning their necks to stare. But they were less than a five minute wonder and soon everyone forgot about them.

Why hadn't their clothes changed? Rosie brooded. Maybe there hadn't been enough power for that. For a couple of minutes she had been terrified of being trapped in the past. Perhaps there had been just enough energy to take two of them through time and for nothing else.

Joseph was looking out the window amazed at the bungalows that had not existed in his world ten minutes earlier. He pointed to a car that passed them. "That's a little bus," he said, becoming more relaxed by the minute.

Behind them, someone overheard and sniggered, but the boy was lost in the view beyond the window.

Rosie sighed. They were still in the countryside and as yet there were not too many obvious or extreme changes. But she knew that soon Joseph would be shocked by the late twentieth century. He would not know what hit him.

Chapter 12

BY THE time they reached the Stillorgan dual carriageway, Joseph's mouth was permanently open. He could not believe the single-span bridges, and he gazed with terror as the traffic passed overhead at Belfield. "Nothing is supporting that bridge!" he said, "What if it falls?"

"It won't."

Rosie was wondering why on earth her clothes hadn't changed. Probably because her visit would be so short it wasn't worth while . . . She felt like a prat and started untying her apron, stuffing the cap into the large front pocket and folding the whole lot up. Beside her, Joseph gave a shout that caused half the bus to jump.

"Shut up," Rosie hissed.

"But look!" His trembling finger was pointing at a huge articulated lorry thundering along the opposite side.

"It's a Guinness lorry," she said. "It's carrying barrels of stout."

He looked at her, "What happened to the horse barges along the Grand Canal?"

"The same as happened to the Dodo. They don't exist any more. Neither does the canal."

"That can't be true! They couldn't get rid of a canal – could they?"

"Well, they haven't exactly got rid of it. But it's very overgrown and there are parts you can't use any more. We're doing a project on it in Geography and – "

This time Joseph's cry caused the bus driver to turn around so that he nearly crashed. The boy had seen an oil tanker and found it terrifying.

The driver seized his microphone, "If that fella down there wearing the peculiar clothes does not see fit to cease shouting and giving a person heart attacks, he will be forcibly ejected from the bus!"

"You'll have to stop screeching," Rosie said, "You sound like one of the Oak Park peacocks. Everyone is looking at us. We might as well go back now if you're going to go on like this."

Joseph was apologetic, "I won't do it again. But things are so strange!"

"They'll be even stranger soon enough," Rosie muttered, certain every passenger on the bus thought she was travelling with a lunatic.

The terminus was at the Liffey. "What time does the bus go to Oak Park in the mornings?" Rosie asked as they were getting off.

"First bus leaves at eight a.m. Why? Is there an asylum in the area? Did they let you out for the day?" The driver laughed loudly at his own joke, then stared at Joseph, "Ah, here son! You're not going to wear that apron around town are you? Do you have your knitting with you as well, by any chance?" Again he cackled.

Rosie pushed the boy down a lane. "He's right. You can't wear that. Take it off and that awful starched collar! That's better. Now you look nearly normal except for the trousers. Still, Mr Murray has a pair like them."

Joseph did not look that much out of place, she thought. Not like her, in her prissy long grey dress, when she should've been wearing jeans and a sweatshirt. She prayed not to meet anyone she knew.

"Now listen," she told him. "We can go home to my house and get a change of clothes. This is Gran's Bridge night and I know Mom and Dad have some sort of business dinner.

They'll be gone out by seven, so we have to stay in town for a while, okay?"

"O-kay," he said, trying out the new word.

"Now, you are going to see a lot of strange things, Joseph, and you can't keep roaring and causing a disturbance. You have to stay cool, not blow it! Okay?"

Rosie's language seemed to have changed with the century, Joseph thought and he struggled to understand.

"I will try not to get hot and to breathe calmly," he said at last.

"What are you talking about? Never mind. Just stay with me and say nothing."

She led him from the comparative safety of the lane into the bedlam of people and traffic. Joseph kept his word, though he stared at the double deckers, the lanes of cars and lorries, the traffic lights, the winking signs, the lights in the shop windows. Rosie would not let him tarry, hurrying him along the crowded pavements until they reached Grafton Street, thronged as usual with shoppers.

She pushed him through the door of MacDonalds. He blinked in the dazzling light. Pointing to a booth she said, "We'll sit there. Now what would you like? A big Mac? Chicken Mac Nuggets? Medium fries, large fries? Milk shake? Raspberry ripple? Chocolate Sundae, Coke?" She stopped.

Joseph hadn't a clue. Best try a word he recognised. "Sunday," He said helpfully.

"It's all right, just wait here."

She was determined he was going to have the treat of his life and came back with Chicken MacNuggets, sweet and sour sauce, a large fries, a coke and a chocolate ice cream sundae.

Doubtfully, he tried the chicken and his eyes widened. He put it down and tasted some chips and beamed. Taking a swig of coke, he caught his breath as the ice hit the back of his throat. He smacked his lips and dipped the plastic spoon into the chocolate sundae, closing his eyes with pleasure.

"You're not supposed to eat them all together," Rosie said, "You take these first, with the coke, then the sundae."

But Joseph kept to his eating pattern, sighing with satisfaction. When he finished he said, "It's different to Mrs Biddle's cooking, but it's nearly as nice."

Now that he was no longer hungry he paid attention to his surroundings. "Are they girls?" he whispered to Rosie, indicating a group in the next booth.

"Of course they're girls! Why do you ask?"

"All females in Oak Park have long hair and would be considered most strange if they wore trousers."

"Those are jeans. A lot of girls and women wear trousers nowadays and have short hair."

His eyes rounded and his voice faltered. "Do gentlemen wear dresses then?"

"No. Of course not. Look at the boys over there. They're not wearing dresses, are they?"

The group of teenagers were not the best example she could have chosen. All of them wore jeans, but one had a magnificent Sioux haircut in rainbow colours, another had long hair, which, when he flicked it back, revealed the shaven sides of his head and a third had a stubble head, like a tennis ball, with the letters "M A C K E R" etched out on the back of his skull. All three wore studs or rings pierced in their noses, lips or eyebrows.

Joseph could not stop looking. The one with "MACKER" on his head caught his eye and stared. Joseph smiled and after a moment the boy grinned and turned back to his mates.

"I would've liked a stud in my nose, only Mom says it's unhygienic," Rosie brooded, "She probably thinks it'd get full of snot. I said I'd have a ring in my bellybutton instead. No one would see that, but she freaked out."

Joseph said nothing, unable to cope with this particular fashion trend.

"Have you ever been to Dublin?" Rosie asked.

"No, but I've seen pictures of Sackville Street. I would like to go there."

"Righto. Only it's called O'Connell Street now."

Joseph made no comment as they made their way, though his head twisted and turned and every now and again he started or clutched her arm. What was ordinary to Rosie was an undreampt of future to him. And it was obvious he felt he was in a different world where nothing was recognisable.

He got his worst fright when they reached College Green and there was a screech of sirens. An escort of police motorbikes swept past leading a cavalcade of dark limousines and garda cars up Dame Street. Overhead a helicopter dipped and hovered, chopping the air with ferocious noise. People sighed and waited, then a few seconds later, surged across the road on their business and the sirens screamed on into the distance.

Joseph was sitting on the ground, hands clenched over his ears, face screwed up in agony. Rosie had no alternative but to sit beside him as no amount of tugging got him to his feet. She sat there waiting, while people walked around them, one or two giving a curious glance at their clothes. One middle-aged man, who barely looked at them, threw tenpence into Rosie's lap, but in general they were ignored.

"We can't sit here forever," Rosie remarked as some of the tension left Joseph. His shoulders stopped hunching and he took his hands down.

"What was that?" he said, "that noise? And that thing in the sky? And all those – whatever – that screeched by?"

"Oh that was just some government people on their way to Dublin Castle." She waved a hand in the general direction and hoped she sounded more knowledgeable than she felt. "See, our government people meet European government people and they all have a sum . . . a sum . . . a *summit* in the castle."

Joseph was not enlightened, "A summit? Like the top of a mountain?"

"No. Not like a top of a mountain. It's a meeting, that's all. And that was a helicopter in the sky. A flying machine."

His face cleared at once. "The butler told me about them. He said a famous writer, Mr Jules Verne, wrote about them."

Rosie nodded and went on to explain about the sirens and motorbikes. When she finished, Joseph had recovered. If Rosie and everyone else accepted such things as normal, then he wasn't in some kind of hell, or worse still, in an alien world. They were only machines. People were more or less the same, only with different fashions.

As they made their way across the Liffey he observed, "People are very tall, much bigger than in Oak Park and they all have shoes. Is everyone rich now, Rosie?"

"No." She pointed to a couple of children begging on the bridge. "Some are very poor."

On O'Connell Street he stopped, his eyes roving up and down.

"What are you looking for?"

"Nelson's Column. Mr Harvey has a collection of Mr Lawrence's views of Dublin. Every photograph of Sackville Street shows Nelson's Column. Mr Harvey says it's a famous landmark."

"Well it's gone. It was blown up."

Now he was staring at the angels around the O'Connell monument.

"What are those holes?"

"Bullet holes. Caused by guns. There was a battle in 1916."

His eyes rounded and Rosie sighed. It would take years to tell him what happened.

"Look, don't worry about them. We haven't time for history lessons – not if you want to see things."

She spent some hours showing him the shops in Henry Street. He was most fascinated when she told him the store they were in was Arnotts.

"Cook and Mrs Smiley mentioned Arnotts. I can hardly believe it is still here." Again he remarked on how well off people were in 1997. "Is it a good time to live?"

Rosie supposed it was. For some people anyway. Better than 1870 and evictions and slaving away for rotten wages.

It was growing dark when they made their way back to O'Connell Street. Joseph stopped and looked at young people down a laneway. They were dazed, staggering, eyes glassy.

"Rosie! What's wrong with them? Are they ill? We should help them."

"No. They're junkies, Joseph. Drug addicts. There's nothing we can do."

Next second they saw a fellow come rushing towards them, crashing against an old lady, knocking her to the ground, then snatching her bag.

Rosie ran to help her up and when she had brushed her down and comforted her, she realised Joseph was gone.

"Oh no . . ." She groaned, but then she saw him racing back waving the bag triumphantly.

"Here you are, madam." The old lady looked astonished, while Joseph rattled on, excited by the small adventure. "Such a stupid fellow, Rosie. When I caught up with him, he poked something at me with a needle at the end of it. When I said I'd like the bag he said he'd give me the needle instead, if I didn't back off. I told him I had no use for a needle and neither had the poor lady he'd illtreated. All she wanted was her bag and he was a fool to think anything else would do!"

Both Rosie and the old lady were open mouthed.

"What are you staring at?" Joseph was uncomfortable. "That fellow looked a bit like you. Couldn't answer me. In the end I just took the bag out of his hand and left him standing there. Of course I told him it wasn't at all manly to knock ladies down. Silly ass!"

"Such a brave fellow," the old lady spoke at last. "Young man, you quite restore my faith in human nature. To take on a thug with a syringe in this day and age. My, my! And you got my bag."

She made the boy take a five pound reward. "I insist.

Young man, I can afford it and will feel badly if you don't accept."

She went off, delighted with herself and especially with Joseph.

He could not resist looking into a dark restaurant in O'Connell Street. Although he could not read, he knew there was something different about the lettering over the door and before Rosie knew what was happening, he had disappeared inside.

When he emerged, his face was bright with delight. "Rosie, there is a Chinese gentleman and young lady in there."

"There would be. It's a Chinese restaurant."

"But I have never met a Chinese person before. I've only seen pictures in the gazette." It seemed to be the biggest adventure of his life.

"We could have something to eat there," she suggested, glad Gran had given her extra money, "in case of emergencies."

She might as well have given him a crock of gold. His excitement was embarrassing. Then she grew more patient. After all, he had travelled 126 years into the future. How would she cope with such a journey? Briefly she wondered what Dublin would be like in the year 2123. She couldn't imagine.

For Joseph, the restaurant was magical.

It was too early for most of the clientele and there were only a few diners. Their table had a snow-white cloth, a candle and a rose. In the background, soft Chinese music played. The waiter set their places and explained the menu. In the end they had Cantonese pork with stirfry vegetables and wild rice. Joseph looked at the red and gold decor, the oriental bronze statues and the prints of the Yangtse river. He sighed.

"Your restaurant is beautiful," he told the waiter, who bowed and said. "Thank you, sir."

When the meal was set before him, Joseph was overcome. "I have never had anything like this before," he said, tasting the pork. "It is delicious, even better than Mrs Biddle's dinners."

Again the waiter bowed and thanked him and brought side dishes of delectable food. "For tasting, sir. No extra charge."

Joseph was in heaven and told the waiter, "You are very kind. Some day I hope to go to China with her majesty's regiment . . . ouch!" Rosie had kicked him, under the table. If he was taken aback, the waiter did not show it. He smiled and brought another dish.

When they had finished, Rosie paid the bill and Joseph asked the waiter, "Tell me, where are you from? Maybe some day I shall visit your homeland!"

"I'm from Santry. Born and bred in Dublin. Sorry to disappoint you sir!" He grinned and Rosie bundled Joseph out onto the street.

It was time to go home.

Chapter 13

WHEN THEY reached Innish Road in Whitehall it was almost eight o'clock. There was no car in the drive and the house was in darkness. Everyone was out. Rosie slipped the key into the lock, opened the door and put on the hall light. Joseph was amazed.

"How did you do that Rosie?" She showed him the switch. For the next few minutes he drove her mad turning on and off the lights downstairs. Eventually she got him to calm down and put him in the sitting-room. "You must stay here and keep quiet, Joseph. I'm going upstairs to change my clothes. I'll get you some of Dad's. If we're going to be around for a while, I don't want to look like a character from a play. I won't be long."

A problem struck her. "Where are we going to sleep?"

She frowned. In all her worrying over Joseph's safety, she had never once thought of this basic problem. They could hardly wander the streets. Then the solution occurred to her. "We could stay here. Not in the house. In the garden shed. It's hardly ever used. I'll get some sleeping bags. Of course we'll have to sneak out in the morning, after they've left. But I think the shed is the best place to stay, don't you?"

It wasn't a very good plan, she thought. Gran and her parents weren't simpletons. They were bound to notice fairly quickly that someone was living in the garden shed. But for the moment it was the best she could come up with.

Joseph wasn't listening. He was looking at the wall lights, the table lamps, the ceiling lights and she knew as soon as she left the room, he was going to try every switch he could find.

Upstairs she rooted through drawers, pulling out sweatshirts and a pair of jeans.

It was obvious from the noises below that Joseph had found the TV switch.

He had pushed the button on the odd looking box and jumped out of his skin when a figure dressed in a white coat appeared and told him, "One of the best cures for backache is to lie on the floor, knees up, feet flat. Try it immediately and feel instant relief."

"I don't have backache," Joseph told the man, "I don't need to lie down."

But the man said earnestly, "Even those who don't suffer from bad backs should try this next exercise."

"Sometimes I get a headache," Joseph said, "I should like a cure for that . . . "

"You may even find," said the man, "that this particular movement can cure other ailments, such as headaches."

"Well, I shall try it when I get home," Joseph said. He noticed a set of smaller buttons on the box and pressed one of them.

"Beware of insecticides," said the lady on the gardening programme. She was dressed very much like himself, in an old shirt and trousers. Behind her was a grove of apple trees. Joseph was interested.

"Chemicals are no substitute for proper organic cultivation. Pesticides are anti-organic." She was frowning, arms folded across her chest in a threatening manner. He could not understand a word. Perhaps the lady was foreign. She looked very cross. He turned a small knob and the lady started shouting at him. Frantic, he ran out of the room.

In the kitchen the first thing he noticed was a bigger box. It was white and had a glass front, a bit like the one in the sitting-room. He could see soapy water behind the glass and what looked like a bundle of fabric. Once again, he was drawn like a magnet to the switch. When he pressed it the machine began to chug, the cloth turning gently in the swishing water. Not very interesting, he thought.

Opening another large white box, he found something he recognised – eggs. Taking one out he was surprised at its coldness, not at all like the eggs he collected from the warm straw in the hen house. Idly passing it from hand to hand, he opened another, smaller box – how many boxes were there in the house? – and seeing a kind of turntable, he put the egg on it, leaving his hands free to twiddle the various knobs. Nothing happened until he shut the door. Then a light came on and he watched through the glass as the egg went round and round. Suddenly there was a loud explosion. The egg was gone!

How strange, he thought. What on earth was the point of a machine that exploded eggs?

Then the washing machine started a spin, the engine whining louder and louder and when he looked, the clothes were a blur, moving so fast he could not have watched them even if he'd wanted to.

Terrified, Joseph ran out of the kitchen, knocking over the plastic bin and the vegetable rack. At the same time Rosie came running onto the landing to see what the racket was.

She was just about to shout down when she heard an angry male adult voice.

"What do you think you're doing, young fellow? You think you can rob the neighbours' house when they're out and no one will notice! Well don't give up the day job. You'd wake up the dead with all those lights going on and off and that terrible rumpus!"

Peering over the banisters, Rosie saw it was Mr Brennan, the man next door. Mom had given him the key so he could keep an eye on things when the house was empty.

Now he made towards Joseph and seized the boy's coat. Joseph, who had frozen for a moment, suddenly sprang into action, unbuttoned his jacket, slipped out of it and ran out the front door. The man ran after him.

Rosie groaned. Mr Brennan had rheumatism and could not get very far but he could ring the police.

She had no time to lose. There was no question of staying in the shed now. And there was no time to change her clothes. But Joseph would need a coat on this chilly night. For that matter so would she. Dashing into her parents' room she rifled the wardrobe.

Dad never wore that old leather jacket, a momento of his youth, kept for the day he'd buy the Harley-Davidson he always craved. The jacket probably didn't even fit him anymore. Rosie swiped it. The noise downstairs was intolerable. If Mr Brennan returned with the police, she would not hear him. In her panic she grabbed the first jacket that came to hand – her mother's. Then she ran, galloping down the stairs, about to hurtle through the door, when the phone rang.

Who was it? Was it the police? Was it another neighbour who might have seen the lights from the house? She lifted the receiver.

"Hello. May I speak to Mr or Mrs McGrath please?"

She recognised Mr Murray's voice. Dear God, what did he want?

"I am afraid they're not in and Gran's not in either," she managed.

"Rosie! Is that Rosie?"

What could she say? "It is I. I mean, it's me, yes. Rosie. Rosie McGrath, if that's who you're looking for."

"Stop dithering, Rosie. I was ringing up to see that you got home safely. The phone in the hostel was out of order. I went to the village to ring, but the storm scuppered the lines. They've only just been fixed. Are you better, Rosie?"

"Oh, yes sir. Thank you, sir. I am completely better. Of course, I'm not better enough to come back hostelling; not *that* better, but I am a lot better. More better than I was."

"You sound deranged," she thought he said.

"I am not deranged!" She was very annoyed.

"I'm sure you're not," he said, surprised.

"So why did you say I was then? That's not very nice. Specially for a teacher."

"Strange. I said you sounded 'strange,' not yourself. Look Rosie, why do you keep shouting at me? Are you sure you're all right?"

"I have to shout 'cos the telly's too loud. But really Mr Murray, I'm fine."

"Just as long you are at home and safe and sound. Now I can stop worrying. Everyone is asking for you. If you're better, maybe you could do a couple of essays for me. Just to keep you from getting bored."

She thought of the man next door and the police and Joseph. Not much chance of boredom. She grew panicky again, "I have to go, sir. Goodbye, sir." She put the phone down. A couple of essays? Teachers weren't normal.

Outside the neighbour was nowhere to be seen. Perhaps he was still following Joseph. Where did the boy go? He'd hardly come back to the house. Mr Brennan must have surely phoned the police by now.

On a hunch she went down to the shops, where the bus stopped, and found Joseph sheltering in a doorway. When she appeared he was radiant with happiness.

"Oh, Rosie, thank goodness. Imagine if I'd never found you again!"

She handed him her father's leather jacket and thought he looked quite handsome when he slipped it on.

"You gave Mr Brennan the slip then?"

"That gentleman? He couldn't catch me. A pity he has my coat. This one is most peculiar."

Rosie was too busy staring at the jacket she'd taken for herself to be indignant. She should have looked at it properly before taking it. Now she was doomed to wear green lurex with red and orange sequins. It was Mom's evening wear and it was gross. It certainly didn't go with the grey dress.

"We have nowhere to sleep," she told Joseph. "And it's freezing. What are we going to do?"

"Go back to Oak Park," he said. He had had enough of the twentieth century. He would rather take his chances in 1870.

"What about Cyril?"

"We'll do our best to stay out of his way. I didn't think of it before we left, everything was so rushed, but Tom Hannigan, the footman, would help us. He has no liking for Master Cyril and I bet he'd find me a proper hiding place. We can ask him in the morning."

"Your trip was a waste of time, Joseph." Rosie felt disappointed for him.

"No, it wasn't. It's been a marvellous experience. It's just that everything is so strange here. And now the police may be after me here too. I'd rather face them in my own time, if I have to."

Rosie nodded, "Let's go then."

But the last bus to Oak Park had left. For a while they sat in the bus station. Then the ticket desk closed and the shutters went down on the shop and a porter told them they'd have to leave. The place would be open to the public at six thirty next morning.

"But we've nowhere to stay," Rosie wailed.

"Well, you can't stay here. Try the family hostel around the corner. It's not pricy. Or try the police station."

They had seven pounds between them, including the five pounds the old lady had given Joseph. It wasn't enough for a hostel and busfares. And if they went to the police, they'd find out all about her and she'd be marched straight back home. Not that they could do the same for Joseph. They'd never believe *his* story. What would happen to him? Maybe he'd be arrested for robbing her house. And she'd be in desperate trouble for skiving off from Outdoor Ed. How would she explain her clothes? Or Mom's horrible jacket?

No, the police station was out of the question.

Seeing her desperate face, the porter thought, not for the first time, how sad it was so many people were homeless, especially youngsters. But it was none of his business. He had his own worries and folk these days didn't always thank you for trying to help. Still these two looked all right, in spite of their funny clothes. "If you're just looking for somewhere to wait till morning, why don't you try the Café Mocha in Stephen's Green? They're open all night."

Rosie could have hugged him.

They took a small out-of-the-way table in the café and no one bothered them. Two cokes lasted for hours. Late night revellers came and went, shift workers, musicians from nightclubs. For a while, Joseph stared at them all, then, like Rosie, he fell into an uneasy slumber.

"Are you all right? You've been asleep for ages." A waitress woke them up.

Rosie looked at her watch, "It's half past six, Joseph. We have to go."

They were the only passengers on the bus and had the same wisecracking driver as the day before. He sniggered at Rosie's jacket. "Stop the lights!" He said. "It's Cinderella coming from the ball."

As she made her way down the aisle, he went into a gag routine over his microphone, "Next we have young Cinders in a green, red and amber evening jacket, bearing a striking resemblance to a set of traffic lights. This is contrasted with a gown of demure grey and a pair of the finest industrial boots."

Rosie thought about going back to kick him with the same stout boots, but did not want to be thrown off the bus.

When they arrived at Oak Park the driver was still in top form. "It's great you were allowed out for the day," he said, "It gives the rest of us a good laugh."

Rosie was fed up with him. "That's more than anyone can say for you, Mister. All you'd ever give a person is a big pain! You should be on the stage, you'd be terrific as a flamin' clown!"

It wasn't respectful, she knew, but then he'd shown her no respect.

The man's good humour evaporated. "You watch it, Miss. You're staying in that hostel, aren't you? Probably with some school. Well, I'm going to make a complaint about you to whatever teacher's in charge. The cheek of you, talking like that!"

Joseph came to her defence immediately, "You are no gentleman," he told the driver. "Mr Harvey says a gentleman always treats people with courtesy, especially all females."

The driver spluttered his annoyance. "The nerve of you, telling me how to behave! In my day a young fella your age knew more than to answer his betters. I bet this Mr Harvey is one of your teachers. Well, I'll be back up here on the afternoon shift and I'll see him then. If I wasn't so late I'd go in now."

Rosie and Joseph got off the bus and the irritated driver moved off, shaking his fist at them.

Again Rosie adjusted her watch, took the necklace pouch out of her dress pocket and clasped it tightly. "Let's decide what to say, Joseph, and then at the count of three, we'll concentrate on nothing else."

After a few moments they fixed on the words.

"Let's keep saying them till they work." Joseph wanted nothing to go wrong this time.

"October 1870. We must get back. To Jane and Lady de Courcy. With the necklace. With all our power."

They chanted the words fervently and on the third try it worked.

The echoes of sound from the start of a busy modern day ceased altogether. The world became more silent as time shifted backwards. To Rosie, there was a slower quality to the morning, the twentieth century rush yielding to an easier pace.

They made their way quietly past the gate lodge and kept close to the trees.

Half way up the drive they were startled when Cyril de Courcy stepped out in front of them. With him were two stalwart constables.

"We have looked everywhere for you," he told Joseph. "And obviously you have been trying to avoid me, trying to escape justice!"

Rosie spoke up. "You mightn't have noticed, Cyril, but we're walking towards the house, not running away from it."

"Sneaking, more like," Cyril spat at her. "We saw how furtive you were."

The constables nodded their solemn agreement. "Skulking with intent," one of them said.

"Exactly!" Cyril was triumphant. "Luckily these two gentlemen were not required at today's eviction. I would have them take you away now, Joseph O'Neill, but my servants must see that villainy will not be tolerated in this household. They must learn that I am their master and cannot be crossed. They must witness your arrest and learn by example what happens to someone like you."

He turned to the policemen. "Take him up to the house. Go through the trees and in the side door at the laundry yard. Keep him in the drawingroom out of sight until the chief constable arrives. He knows there may be trouble and will bring reinforcements. On his arrival, I shall summon the servants."

Should he make a run for it? Joseph hesitated and looked at Rosie. In a second the two men had gripped his arms and were leading him through the trees.

"Don't worry!" Rosie shouted after him. "I'll sort it out!"

"No you won't!" But Cyril was talking to himself. Rosie was flying up the drive. About to take after her, Cyril checked himself. The constables had searched her room less than half an hour ago and had found nothing. There was no point following her, unless the diamonds were on her person and he doubted it. She was only a skivvy and obviously did not have the nerve or the brains to hide a priceless necklace. Why demean himself running after her? She was unimportant.

Chapter 14

ROSIE REACHED the house well before the police and their prisoner. She slipped up the backstairs to her room without meeting anyone. She had to put the necklace back at once. If the police found it there was a chance Joseph would go free.

But first she must make sure the coast was clear. Stuffing the necklace under her mattress, she sped down the stairs and corridors to Lady de Courcy's room on the first landing. Her face fell and her steps slowed when she saw Miss Payne outside.

"What are *you* doing here?" The governess said. "Skivvies are not allowed in this part of the house, not unless they are carrying coal buckets, or logs or performing other menial tasks."

"What are you doing here?" Rosie countered.

Miss Payne flushed. "Such impudence. I do not answer to the lower orders."

But the question set her brooding. "As you well know, my place is with Miss Florence. But apparently my services are not required. That thief's sister is to be her companion. Literature and Mathematics are to be abandoned until they return." She sniffed. "It is not a policy with which I agree. I should be with her now. Young Jane cannot teach sums, can she? Or talk to her about Mr Tennyson and Mr Dickens."

Not for the first time, it occurred to Rosie that Miss Payne was actually fond of Florence and missed her company. She was lonely. But her reference to Joseph as a thief left Rosie with little sympathy. Serve the woman right. She treated the servants without respect, not wanting their friendship. They were kind and generous and Miss Payne had no time for them.

"Well, don't hover idly by, girl! Go about your tasks." The governess's voice was sharp. "Or have you some purpose here? Some little errand to perform for that thief, presuming he has come out of hiding. Perhaps the necklace is in your pocket."

She advanced on Rosie, who stepped back hastily. "No it isn't. Look!" She turned out the two deep pockets of her dress. Miss Payne was disappointed and scanned the girl for a sign of some other hiding place. None came to mind. The governess got quite cross. "You are a most disgraceful skivvy," she said. "You are not wearing your apron or cap and your appearance is woeful."

When Rosie said nothing, the governess dismissed her in disgust. "Disappear at once girl. Master Cyril will be arriving any moment and he finds your kind utterly distasteful."

Rosie went.

So Cyril was meeting Miss Payne. That should be interesting. Two villains discussing their plot. Such a conversation would be worth hearing.

Then Rosie caught her breath as two ideas occurred to her. Two beautiful, simple ideas. She was a genius! Rushing up to the attic quarters, she slipped into Jane's bedroom and took her rucksack from its hiding place.Once back in her own room, she rummaged feverishly till she found the tape recorder. Then she took the necklace from under the mattress. Now she was ready.

She knew Mrs Smiley's directions to the short corridor off by heart. "At the school room, turn right, go down the next set of steps and left again."

In no time Rosie found herself back in front of the wooden panelling. Firmly she pressed the centre of the curved rose.

Once again the panel shifted back and Rosie was hurrying down the secret passage. Once again she turned the heavy knob and felt the bookcase move. Cautiously she pushed, so that inch by inch it creaked open, and she was in Lady de Courcy's bedroom. Swiftly she crept over to the dressing-table and slid the pouch along the floor behind it.

Outside was the murmur of voices and Rosie knew Cyril had arrived. The door was too thick for her to make out the conversation, even with her ear pressed against it.

Taking a deep breath she turned the handle and drew the door back a fraction. It made no sound, hinges smoothly oiled. Now the voices were clear and Rosie pressed the "record" button on her tape recorder. Peering out, she could see only Cyril, who had his back to her, blocking Miss Payne from view. Her words, however, were very plain.

"The boy has not appeared so far, Master Cyril. But he must have the necklace and I cannot understand why he has not yet tried to replace it. Unless of course, he actually decides to keep it . . ."

"Even if he wished to, he could not put the jewels back now, Miss Payne. He is at the moment in the drawing-room, in the custody of two constables. I found him sneaking around the drive."

Oh God. This wouldn't convince anyone that Joseph was innocent. Rosie felt despair. Then her spirits soared.

"Are you sure you put the diamonds in his room?" Cyril's voice was waspish.

"Certain! I have made no mistake," Miss Payne was aggrieved. "I followed your instructions to the letter, Master Cyril. While you were giving him the butterflies, I brought the necklace to his room. There was a wooden box there, on his table, with the letter 'J' on it. J for Joseph. I put the diamonds in it. The whole exercise took about five minutes. Perfectly executed." She sniffed.

"So perfectly executed the diamonds haven't been seen since!" Cyril was distinctly ratty. "So perfectly executed that my exquisite collection of butterflies was buried under a tree and ruined. I blame you for this, Miss Payne."

It was not the right tone to take. "Blame me? Blame me? Blame yourself! Only a fool would have given such a priceless collection to an idiot boy in the first place."

Cyril was breathing hard. "And only a foolish servant would have botched up the simple task of transferring a necklace from one room to another."

He had gone too far. Miss Payne was furious. "I am an educated lady, Master Cyril. Your mother employed me as a governess, not as a servant."

"There is no difference." His tone was as nasty as he could make it. "You will never be one of us, Miss Payne, never dine with us, entertain with us, or converse with us on an equal level."

Silence.

Rosie thought they had finished and was about to switch off the machine. Then she heard Miss Payne's low voice. "You are right, Master Cyril. I am indeed nothing but a foolish servant. No one but a fool would have done what I did. I can see now there will be no reward for me in this venture and it would be just as well to inform Lady de Courcy of the true circumstances of the missing jewels. Your mother is a kind-hearted woman. No doubt she will forgive a foolish mistake made by a foolish servant. Especially when she witnesses my remorse."

Her words threw Cyril into a panic. At once he was apologetic, even fawning. "You have misunderstood me, my dear Miss Payne. I merely wished to point out your position as it stands now, not as it will be when we have rid the house of these sly peasants. Mother will appreciate our efforts to unmask them. I shall *make* her appreciate me. Then you will have your just reward."

After a few more seconds the tape clicked to a stop. Rosie had heard enough. Better to go while they were still talking. She eased the door shut, put the machine in her pocket and made her way to the kitchen.

The butler was just leaving as Rosie came in. "Hi, Mr Harvey," Rosie spoke without thinking.

"High? What's high?" But he was distracted by other matters and went on his way. Cook was sitting at the table and did not give out about Rosie's extraordinary time-keeping.

"I heard you kept young Joseph company yesterday," she said. "And now Mr Harvey says two polis are guarding him in the drawing-room. Is he in a terrible state?"

"Not really. I told him everything will be fine."

"Your brain must be addled so. How could everything be fine with the polis arresting him for stealing a priceless necklace? Mr Harvey thinks he should try to escape. Take his chances and run."

"No, he shouldn't," Rosie was earnest. "If he ran, Cyril would say that proved he was guilty. Then he'd get rid of Jane, somehow. Joseph would never see his sister again. He didn't take the necklace, Mrs Biddle. He shouldn't leave."

"Sure I know he didn't take the necklace, but what's that to do with anything? Master Cyril hates his bones."

After a silence, Rosie changed the subject. She wanted to ask Mrs Biddle a favour, and it had to be tackled delicately.

"Yesterday Joseph was saying what he'd like to do when he's a man."

"Well, I'm sure it's not part of his plans to spend time in Van Diemens' Land."

"It is not." Rosie had no idea who Van Diemen was, but wanted to get to the point as carefully as she could. "He doesn't want to spend his time on the land at all, Mrs Biddle. He wants to join the army in a couple of years and be a captain of a regiment. He wants to travel the world."

"He has no hope." Mrs Biddle was blunt.

"That's what I was thinking, unless he could read and write. Then he might get promoted."

"No, he wouldn't. He'd have to buy a commission and only rich men can do that. Poor men remain ordinary soldiers. They stay poor."

"But that's not fair! There must be some way . . ."

"Oh indeed. If he saved his general's life he might, just might, become a corporal."

Rosie dredged up a fact she'd learned recently in History. "Wasn't Napoleon once a corporal? He became an emperor."

Mrs Biddle stared at her, "You are a very strange skivvy," she said. "I have never been given a history lesson by a scullery maid before."

Rosie went on hastily, "You're always saying how great it is to be able to read and write. Well, if Joseph joins the army and he can't do either, he'll never get anywhere and what's more he won't be able to keep up proper contact with Jane, just like you and your brother."

Mrs Biddle viewed her through narrowed eyes.

"What exactly do you want, Rosie?"

"I thought maybe the two of them, Joseph and Jane, could learn from Mr Harvey. He could teach them when he's teaching you."

Mrs Biddle looked at a spot on the wall, "So the gardener's boy and his sister will know I can't read and write. I might as well announce it to the whole world. In fact when the constabulary arrives, I think I'll stand on the stairs with Master Cyril and tell the assembled servants that Mrs Biddle does not know her letters!" Her expression was grimly amused.

"Please, Cook. They'd keep it a secret."

Rosie looked so disappointed, Mrs Biddle gave in. "There now, don't fret! I'm tired of keeping it a secret myself, Rosie. If Mr Harvey doesn't mind, why should I care what anyone else thinks? Maybe I *should* announce it from the stairs. So yes, I'll ask Henry if he'll help those two. That's if Joseph isn't taken away by the polis. Just now he has more to worry about than learning his letters. Anyway, why wouldn't you give them a hand yourself?"

"I won't be able to. I mean, with all the work I've to do. Anyway, Mr Harvey'd be much better. He's so clever. He'd be able to explain even the hardest words."

"He would, wouldn't he? I'll put in a word for them so."

For quite a while now a question had been niggling at the back of Rosie's mind and at lunchtime she decided to look for an answer. "Mr Harvey!" She called. The butler was engrossed in conversation with Mrs Biddle and did not hear. She waved her hand a few times, then, not the most patient of people, she yelled "Mr Harvey! I want to ask you something."

The table went completely silent and she realised at once that this was not acceptable behaviour for a scullery maid. But she wasn't a scullery maid, was she? She was Rosie McGrath and she was sick of 1870 where she was some sort of freak if she opened her mouth to ask a question.

Mr Harvey frowned and shook his head. He was shaking his head so much, Rosie thought it might actually swivel right around.

It was Cook who answered, "Ask away, Rosie. Mr Harvey'll be only too delighted to share his vast store of knowledge."

The butler's head stopped in mid-shake and he looked astonished. So did the rest of the servants. But he did not want to displease Mrs Biddle, so he nodded graciously at Rosie.

"I was wondering why Cyril is so mean to the servants. Why does he hate them so much?"

"*Master* Cyril to you child. I fear your career as a scullery maid will not last long."

"Oh, I don't mind, Mr Harvey. To tell you the truth I hate the job!" Rosie'd had enough criticism.

"Answer the child's question," Mrs Biddle averted friction.

The butler cleared his throat. Everyone was waiting. Most of them knew the reason for Cyril's hatred but wanted to see how Mr Harvey would cope with the sorry tale.

"When Master Cyril was younger," the butler began, "his great friend was his cousin, Francis Millsworth, heir to the Millsworth estate in County Tipperary. Master Cyril spent a lot of holidays on that estate and was fond of his aunt and uncle, Lord and Lady Millsworth. He did not dislike servants then."

The butler reflected a moment and Rosie wondered where all this was leading. "In fact, he often spoke of a young manservant, Jack Farrell, engaged by Lord Millsworth to look after his son and the young visitor during the long vacation. Jack Farrell taught them hurling and Gaelic football. He took them in the pony trap on picnics, or climbing in the mountains. He was an energetic young man and the two boys thought the world of him. Master Cyril became less timid, more frank and manly."

The silence around the table was acute as the butler's story reached its point.

"The last summer Master Cyril spent there was three years ago, some months before the Fenian Rising. He was looking forward to seeing his cousin and Farrell again. But Farrell had changed. He was surly and ill-mannered towards his charges, unwilling to fulfil his duties."

Again the butler stopped, looking at his audience. The servants' faces were expressionless and he went on, "One day Farrell was to drive the two boys and Lord and Lady Millsworth in the family brougham to some grand occasion in Tipperary town. A few days before he had asked for extra wages and Lord Millsworth had refused. Then he had shouted at his Lordship over evictions and unfair rents, affairs which were none of his business."

It was clear from the expressions on the faces on those around the table that they were not in agreement. But nothing was said.

"Lord Millsworth should have instantly dismissed him, but he was a kind man . . . "

At this there was a snort from the others and the butler amended, "On this occasion at least, he was a kind man. He knew of his son's fondness for Farrell and that swayed his judgement."

The footman, Mr Hannigan, stood up abruptly. "Mr

Harvey, I have great respect for you but I cannot listen to this any longer. Lord Millsworth was a bad landlord, a rack renter, evicting his tenants on the slightest excuse. Many of them finished their days in the workhouse, buried in paupers' graves. He cleared the land during the Great Hunger, when families were so poor and starving they could not meet his rents. A 'kind man' he was not!" With that he stalked from the room and the butler cleared his throat once more.

"All I know is that, on this occasion, he did not dismiss his servant, although greatly provoked.

"At the appointed time Farrell drove the family and Master Cyril towards Tipperary. Five miles from home, at a spot where the road is hidden from view by trees and shrubbery, Farrell stopped the carriage. In an instant it was surrounded by a dozen or so Ribbon men, and the family was dragged out. Lord Millsworth, his wife and son were shot dead. Apparently, Farrell asked them not to kill Francis, but he was reminded of his oath. There could be no going back."

The butler swallowed, unable to stomach the horror.

"And Cyril?" Rosie whispered.

"They left Master Cyril alive to tell the story, so that there would be no doubt who did it and why. 'Tell your father' they said, 'tell everyone you meet, what you saw here this evening so they know landlords will pay a high price for their injustice.'"

No one spoke. Not even a murmur. At last Mr Harvey sighed. "It was then Master Cyril changed. Since that time he has no trust in any of us. His father's death some months afterwards did not help matters. These last few years he has been determined to show who is lord and master."

"What are Ribbon men, Mr Harvey?"

"A secret society of men who have sworn to kill those who stand in the way of what they call freedom. Even Fenians would not condone their methods."

Rosie pondered. Cyril had seen three people murdered in cold blood. He had lost his best friend. A man he liked and trusted had conspired to kill them. Now he was afraid and trusted no one, except his mother and sister.

And he could not bear any servant to have a place in their affections.

"What happened to Jack Farrell?" Rosie said.

"He was brought to trial and executed."

At that moment Mr Hannigan, the footman, returned to announce, "Master Cyril wants everyone in the hall. The chief constable and his men have arrived."

"Glory be to God," Cook muttered. "We're spending more time in that hall these days than anywhere else."

Chapter 15

CYRIL DID not want his "enemy" to be quietly taken away. He wanted him humiliated as publicly as possible, led away in handcuffs in the presence of the servants. To that end he had summoned even the outdoor workers to the front hall.

He stood midway on the stairs, flanked by two policemen, the chief inspector behind him and four more stalwarts a few steps down. He was addressing an audience of more than eighty servants. At the front of the crowd stood Joseph, one policeman at his side, the other at the back of the crowd, in front of the great door. Tom Hannigan, head footman, stood behind Joseph.

The footman spoke in a low voice, "If there's a move to arrest you lad, be ready to slip back and out the front door. You'll find it open."

"What about this fellow?" Joseph murmured, indicating the large policeman.

"Leave him to us. There are plenty of strong men behind you. They know what to do. Everyone here knows you're not a robber, but that won't stop Master Cyril. So, when the time comes, you make a dash for it."

As a last resort he would run, Joseph thought, but perhaps he would not have to, if Rosie had put back the necklace.

Every servant went still when Cyril held up his hand to speak.

"I have summoned you all here, so that you may witness

the arrest of one of your own and know that no one can get away with villainy in this house." There wasn't a stir.

"Joseph O'Neill has robbed a priceless necklace."

The servants stared silently at Cyril and their stillness unnerved him so that his voice shook slightly as he continued, "This necklace was a precious gift to my mother from her husband, my father, Lord de Courcy. She trusted this boy, Joseph, and he repaid her trust with dishonesty and meanness."

Below him on the stairs the four policemen shifted uncomfortably. They liked neither the total silence nor the expressions of the crowd. At Joseph's side, the large man in uniform began to sweat. He ran a finger round the inside off his stiff collar.

"There was a witness to this robbery and there can be no doubt as to the culprit. Therefore I order the arrest of Joseph O'Neill."

"Joseph is innocent," Rosie piped up, her words clear in the dead silence.

She should have spoken sooner.

Already Tom Hannigan had pulled the boy back and a passage was cleared between the crowd. Already the police were moving after him and shouting. Joseph was powerless to stop the hands eagerly assisting him. In seconds, he found himself facing the wide open door. The crowd closed behind him, hampering the men in uniform. The large policeman who had been guarding him drew out a baton. Tom Hannigan gripped his arm, "Don't be a fool. You'll start a riot."

But the big man foresaw trouble from his inspector. He shook off the footman and raised the baton. Skillfully Hannigan tripped him and the policeman stumbled. The baton was wrested from his grip and disappeared. Afterwards he could never say for certain who was responsible.

Reluctant to leave without even attempting to clear his name, Joseph found he had no choice. Trying to turn back, he was twisted round again and set on a forward course. The force of those behind him was unstoppable. There was no reasoning with them. He could not make his voice heard above the shouting. He might as well run.

But as the crowd surged through the front door, a carriage drew up at the steps and, not waiting for assistance, Lady de Courcy alighted, followed by Miss Florence and Jane.

The pushing stopped and Lady de Courcy stared at the servants.

"What on earth is happening?" she said.

"It's her Ladyship!"

"Tell her what happened."

Everyone spoke at once. Lady de Courcy was deafened.

Mr Harvey, who had not been part of the mad scramble and who had stepped up the stairs to get a better view, called for order. So did the police inspector – to no avail. Word came back to him that her ladyship was outside and could not get into her own house. It was then that the inspector, in the belief that her life was in danger, fired his pistol into the air and everything went quiet.

The servants cleared a way for Lady de Courcy and followed her back into the hall, with Jane and Florence in the midst of the crowd.

She made her way towards the inspector who was holding the smoking weapon.

"How dare you set off your pistol in my house, frightening my servants and ruining my ceiling." She saw her son on the stairs, took in the other policemen and at once knew what was happening.

In a moment she was beside Cyril and her angry voice rang through the hallway.

"It is as well I came home unexpectedly, Cyril. I left strict orders for nothing to be done until my return. Why did you not obey them?"

Cyril flushed at the reprimand. "Because mother, that thief was about to escape. You saw him make the attempt, did you not?"

There was dead silence as Lady de Courcy digested this and Cyril looked triumphant.

"That's not fair!" This time Rosie's voice held everyone's attention and she rushed on, "None of us thinks Joseph is a thief."

There was a murmur of agreement, but she did not want to be interrupted. "Maybe the necklace wasn't found because no one looked in the right place."

She had their interest now. Lady de Courcy was frowning. Mr Harvey said, "I really must apologise for the scullery maid, My Lady. The girl has no sense of her place in this establishment. Indeed, she has no sense whatsoever. She does not realise that she is not allowed to speak to her betters in this way. In fact she does not realise she must not speak to them at all, unless they address her first."

"Listen to her, Mother. Please." It was Florence.

"Let her have her say, I will listen," Her Ladyship said and Rosie put her case.

"You went all panicky when your necklace was missing. Did you ever search your own room? I mean, it could be there, you know. Somewhere or other."

"It's definitely not in your room. Mother . . ." Cyril got no further.

Lady de Courcy said, "How do you know that? I never looked there. Did you?"

Caught off guard, Cyril shook his head and his mother continued, "The girl is right. When I realised the necklace was not in its usual place, I could not think properly. We should have searched the room and must do so now, at once. Come with me." She summoned the two policemen. "The rest of you stay here. You as well, Cyril."

While she was gone, there was silence in the great hall, the tension rising. Rosie prayed that the necklace would be found and smiled encouragingly at Joseph, who was pale and drawn.

All the time Cyril looked impatient, certain nothing would come of this search.

But within five minutes Lady de Courcy was back again, holding the diamonds up for all to see.

"The necklace was not stolen at all! It had fallen at the back of the dressing table and was wedged behind one of the legs. I must apologise to every one of you . . ."

Cyril's mouth dropped. Then his amazement turned to rage. "You are very naïve, Mother! You forget Miss Payne saw Joseph O'Neill with the diamonds. If they are now back in your room then somehow, he put them back – or that wretched scullery maid."

There were cries of "Shame!" "Not true!" from the servants, but Rosie could see Lady de Courcy was swayed by the logic of her son's words. She had forgotten the witness. Rosie longed for silence so she could play her trump card. Lady de Courcy raised a hand so she could question the girl further and in the hush that followed, Rosie played the preset tape.

"Are you sure you put the diamonds in his room?"

"Certain. I have made no mistake. I followed your instructions to the letter, Master Cyril. While you were giving him the butterflies, I brought the necklace to his room."

The voices were crystal clear, recognisable at once. The effect was extraordinary. Servants strained to look at Cyril and Miss Payne and could not believe that neither were in fact speaking. Cyril was deathly pale, while at the foot of the stairs Miss Payne gripped the banisters, half fainting.

The disembodied voices went on, yet it was obvious the two speakers were in no fit state to say anything. Neither was anyone else, with the exception of Rosie. The hall was acoustically perfect and the powerful tape projected the sound everywhere. No one noticed the small object in Rosie's hand. No one realised she had anything to do with the voices. All of them were terrified, especially Miss Payne.

When the tape stopped, she became hysterical.

"It's true. All of it. Master Cyril hates the boy and his sister. But those voices – they are ours. We said those words earlier this morning! Now they have come back to haunt us. This is our punishment!"

Rosie slipped the tape back into her pocket. There was no way she could explain it.

Lady de Courcy stared at her son. His head was bowed.

When at last she spoke, her voice shook. "Miss Payne is telling the truth, Cyril, isn't she?" He nodded.

"Why did you do it?"

"Because you think too much of Joseph O'Neill. I keep telling you we cannot trust him, or his kind."

"It is *you* I cannot trust Cyril. *You* who lied and cheated. You would have had this defenceless boy arrested, imprisoned, separated from his sister. You are jealous and scheming."

Cyril could not look at her. Humiliated, he stared at the ground and muttered, "You have your necklace back. What else matters?"

"You cannot think I take any pleasure from it, after what you have done. I would rather your poor father had never given it to me!"

Her hands trembled as she put the diamonds back in the pouch. Then she straightened and turned to those below.

"I must apologise to all of you for my son's behaviour, especially towards young Joseph whom I will see later. As for you, Miss Payne, you may pack your bags at once. There is no place for you here. Mr Harvey, will you see to it that the constabulary partake of some hospitality before they depart?" She turned away.

Was Cyril to get off scot free, Rosie wondered, with nothing more than a scolding and reprimand? His mother could hardly press charges of robbery against him, but surely the inspector could do something.

The inspector had the same idea. "Madam," he called, "There is the matter of your son."

She stopped, a few steps above Cyril, who had not moved.

"I shall deal with my son, Inspector."

"No doubt you will my Lady, but so must I. He has conspired

against an innocent lad and he has wasted valuable police time. My men will escort him to the barracks for questioning."

Lady de Courcy put a hand to her heart. It was clear she was shocked. The Inspector quickly went up to her. He spoke quietly and after a moment, Rosie saw the colour come back into her face and she nodded.

Without protest, Cyril was led away by two constables. The servants disbanded in silence, still amazed and disturbed by those mysterious voices.

Jane came across to Rosie. "Thank you for speaking up," she said before following Florence out of the hall.

Rosie's task was accomplished but she could not go home until she had seen Joseph. Cook and Mrs Smiley kept her busy for the rest of the day, scrubbing and cleaning. She polished the Benares brass figurines and scraped the grit out of the wrinkles in the huge elephant foot. It was used as an umbrella stand and, like the brass, was a memento of Lord de Courcy's years in the Indian Army.

There was much talk among the servants about the day's events and much puzzlement about the tape.

"Their voices were as clear as day, yet they weren't speaking!"

"You knew it was them all right, yet there was something strange about the sound. It was ghostly."

"But you can't be a ghost when you are still alive. It doesn't make sense."

"It was God. He did it!"

"I never heard of God imitating voices before. That's daft."

On and on the argument went. Rosie was tempted to take out the little machine and press it under their noses, but that would lead to awkward questions.

She finally saw Joseph at dinner. When all were seated Mr Harvey tapped a spoon against a glass and said, "Lady de Courcy wishes to make amends for this afternoon. She says we are to drink to Joseph's health and has supplied us with wine and porter. We are at liberty to enjoy ourselves, and her ladyship has insisted that we have the rest of the evening free."

There was a cheer from the table. Quickly the glasses were filled, home-made lemonade for the younger servants, alcohol for the rest.

Mr Harvey proposed a toast, "To young Joseph and to her Ladyship!"

Soon, the butler stood again, "To Cook for her magnificent beauty and charm." Cook blushed and after the first astonishment everyone clapped and shouted approval.

There were more toasts:

"To young Rosie for speaking up!"

"To one and all here present for never doubting Joseph!"

"To the polis and Lady de Courcy for finding the necklace!"

Some discussion of the day's extraordinary events followed, everyone eager to have their say, while the glasses were drained and refilled at an alarming rate.

Then Mr Harvey was on his feet once more, this time quite sentimental and a little tipsy, "Cook deserves more toasts! To a wonderful, perfect woman and the best cook ever. She is as beautiful as her own apple tart. To Mrs Biddle, to glorious spacious Honoria Stacia, soon to be Mrs Henry Harvey!"

This time Cook went puce and covered her face. But Mr Harvey made her stand and take a bow and when she sat again, Tom Hannigan, the head footman, stood up and shouted "Hooray for Mrs Biddle and Mr Harvey!" and raised his glass. Everyone followed suit.

Afterwards, the table was cleared and pushed back. Accordions, violin and flute appeared. Without prompting Jane stood beside the three musicians.

Tom Hannigan called for the first tune, "'Just a Song at Twilight,' Mrs Biddle's favourite. She and Mr Harvey might waltz if they have a mind."

There was a hush as the melody began, sweetly played, accompanying Jane's pure voice.

Rosie was overcome with a kind of sadness. Soon she'd be gone, leaving behind the warm kitchen and soft lamplight. She would never see any of these people again.

She would never get to know Jane well, never see Cook and Mr Harvey's marriage, never know what lay ahead for Tom Hannigan or Mrs Smiley. Her life had touched only briefly on theirs.

Mr Harvey took Mrs Biddle's hand and they waltzed, Cook a little self-conscious at first, then losing herself in the music. They were so proud of each other, their delight obvious.

The sight of anyone older than twenty dancing usually sent Rosie into fits of giggles. But this, she thought, was beautiful. Not a bit like Mam and Dad's mortifying efforts at rock 'n' roll.

Then Mrs Smiley shrieked her way through "I dreamt I dwelt in Marble Halls" and Rosie was no longer quite so sad at the thought of leaving. A few more mugs of porter and Tom Hannigan announced, "This song is for Allen, Larkin and O'Brien – dead these three years."

Proudly he stood, hand on heart and sang:

"*God save Ireland say the heroes*
God save Ireland say we all
Whether on the scaffold high
Or the battlefield we die,
Oh what matter, when for Erin dear we fall . . ."

It was the only verse he knew and he sang it three times with great passion.

This was followed by some ceili music and more dancing. Joseph did a slip jig on the huge table with everyone clapping in time. He was the centre of much attention. Every time he tried to have a serious conversation with Rosie, someone interrupted to talk about the day's events and she hardly got to speak to him.

"Joseph is very eager to talk to you," Jane said. She had been watching them for some time.

"I suppose he wants to thank me for saying Lady de Courcy should look in her room."

Rosie wished she could tell her all that had happened and explain that Joseph knew she must soon be on her way to her own time. But she was quite certain Jane would think she was mad.

"He is right to thank you." And suddenly she hugged Rosie. "Mr Harvey was shocked when you spoke up. Everyone was. You might have lost your place. You are very brave."

"Not as brave as you. You helped that night in the stable when I could do nothing." Rosie was also remembering Gran's stories of Jane's harsh life.

At least now Jane would not lose her brother. Nor would she be penniless and alone on the steets of Dublin.

"You saved Joseph from prison, Rosie. I'll remember that and you'll always be my friend."

Rosie could say nothing. The words filled her with a sense of loss. Jane did not belong to her future. They would never see each other again and she could never explain why. There was no hope of friendship.

The party finished around midnight and Joseph at last caught up on Rosie outside her bedroom door. "I don't know how you managed Cyril's and Miss Payne's voices," he told her. "You must be a genius and I'm very grateful."

Rosie thought it an immense pity she could only be a genius in the distant past.

"It's great everything worked out, Joseph. Now I can go home. I'll get the eleven o'clock bus tomorrow."

He nodded, his eyes sad. "Tomorrow is the tenants' day for calling on Lady de Courcy. They usually arrive mid-morning. You'll have to be gone by then. Mrs Brannigan always visits to pay her respects and someone is bound to say something about her daughter."

As she opened the door into her room, Joseph touched her arm. "I shall miss you, Rosie. We must talk again before you leave. Promise not to go without seeing me."

Rosie smiled agreement.

Tomorrow she was going home, and in one way the prospect terrified her. She sensed that the journey through time with Joseph had required more energy than ever before. What if her powers were drained? What if she did not make it home? The alternative was terrifying.

Chapter 16

ALL NIGHT she tossed and turned, wide awake, and as soon as dawn filtered through the window she got up, not waiting for the gong.

Mrs Biddle was already in the kitchen.

"Well, aren't you the early riser, Rosie. I suppose you're like myself, couldn't sleep after last night's excitement. Help yourself to some breakfast." In spite of her anxiety, Rosie found the porridge very tasty. At home she wouldn't eat it, despite Mom's insistence on its goodness. "When I was your age, Rosie, I always ate porridge. It puts the lining in your stomach." Rosie imagined the cement-like substance Mom created hardening into concrete walls inside her and refused. But Mrs Biddle's porridge was delicious and Rosie gladly had a second helping.

"Your mother will be pleased to see you today Rosie, after the tenants' meeting. I've no doubt she misses you."

Rosie mumbled and Cook went on, "She must be very proud of you, able to read and write, the clever one of the family."

She must go and congratulate Mrs Brannigan today, Cook thought. Tell her what a great girl her daughter was.

In fact it was beyond all understanding, she mused. The Brannigans were not famous for their brains. Quite the opposite. That Rosie was a Brannigan defied the laws of nature. Sipping a cup of tea, Cook studied the girl. Fair hair, brown eyes, heart shaped face. The Brannigans had glorious flame-coloured hair, blank blue eyes and freckled faces. This girl hadn't one freckle, just a solitary pimple beside her nose. Rosie caught Cook's gaze and touched the spot. She loathed pimples and this one had appeared overnight. It must be enormous to have Cook staring at it.

"Where did you come from?" Mrs Biddle said.

Rosie flushed and her heart skipped a beat. "You don't look like a Brannigan," Cook mused, eyes narrowing.

Was she going to accuse her of impersonation? What did she know?

Desperately Rosie said, "I'm like my Gran – and my great-grandmother." She hoped there were no Brannigan grannies hanging around.

Mrs Biddle had to be satisfied. "Well, I suppose there's no accounting for the fact that looks, and in your case brains, can skip generations." Then she smiled warmly and went on, "I never thanked you for all you did. I wouldn't have had any courage without you. And to think Mister Harvey doesn't care whether I can read or write. He says I'm clever, Rosie. D'you think maybe he's deluded? A bit soft in the head?"

"He's soft about you," Rosie said. "And anyway reading and writing isn't clever. I know an awful lot of people who can read and write, but they can't add up in their head like you can and they can't remember extremely long and boring lists like you can. They have nothing in their brains."

She stopped. Cook was looking at her strangely. "What's wrong?" Rosie faltered. You'd think she had two heads the way Cook was staring. Was it her pimple? Maybe it was grotesque? She fingered the spot.

"What do you mean, you know a lot of people who can read and write?"

"Did I say that? Probably I mean . . ." Rosie picked her way carefully, "Probably I mean I know *about* such people, reading about them and that."

Cook was still looking. "Probably you do," she murmured, unconvinced.

Rosie changed the subject. It was time to say good-bye. Rising from the table she said, "I have to get started. Thank you so much for the breakfast, Mrs Biddle, and for all your food. I hope you and Mr Harvey will be very happy. Your porridge is beautiful and in all my life I won't forget you."

Mrs Biddle was used to people being overcome by her cooking. It seemed to bring out formal speeches in everyone. She nodded and smiled. Such a well mannered girl!

Rosie was at the door when Mrs Smiley entered. "So there you are," said the housekeeper, out of breath as usual. "I declare I don't know how you do it!"

"Do what?" Rosie said.

"Disappear, girl, disappear! My ears are shattered looking for you. I reached your room just as that blooming gong went. It shuddered through my entire self, and me after climbing all them stairs. And then you weren't there, girl!" She glared at Rosie, holding her responsible for all her early morning trauma. Gripping the girl's arm in case she vanished once more, Mrs Smiley told her, "Miss Florence wants to see you, in the schoolroom."

"Right, I'll go now." Mrs Smiley's grip was a vice.

"No you shan't. Stop wiggling about, girl. Miss Florence is having her breakfast just now and won't be in the schoolroom for another hour. She feels bad, poor love, over yesterday's events. Why she wants to see someone who behaves like a vanishing eel is beyond me. Mind you don't upset her."

"I won't, Mrs Smiley . . ." Rosie hesitated. She wanted to make her farewells without giving herself away. "Mrs Smiley, you've been very nice to me. And your singing last night was very . . . very . . ." Finding the right word was difficult, "really very interesting. So I'd like to wish you well."

"Wish me well! But I ain't goin' nowhere. Though you're right about my singing. I were once told by an impresario that my voice has a most powerful effect on people. He dropped dead just half an hour later, poor man."

Rosie gasped, "My God! You must have been very upset."

"Indeed I were. I might've had a career in music hall but for that. With such talent I might even have been in the opera."

Rosie nodded. At least the world had been spared Mrs Smiley.

"Well, thanks for everything," she said.

The housekeeper's grip slackened, but Rosie had to give her a little push to loosen it completely. She was out the door before Mrs Smiley recovered.

Time was passing and she had to see Joseph. She made her way to his room. Luckily he was still there. "Mr Harvey told me I could have a free morning," he said.

Rosie got to the point, "Joseph, you know the trouble we had making our journeys. I'm afraid the same thing will happen again and I won't be able to get home."

He paled on her account, remembering his own fright at the thought of being trapped forever in an alien world. Then he said, "I'll help you, Rosie. If we both concentrate on you going home, maybe you'll succeed."

"But what if you're carried along with me? You're taking a big risk."

"No, I'm not." He tried to sound convincing. "You said it yourself. There won't be the power to take the two of us. It's worth a try." She nodded and relaxed a little.

"Did you get to see Lady de Courcy yet?"

His face brightened. "Yes, Rosie, she is very kind. She told me I must be compensated for what Master Cyril did and asked me what I most wanted in life. When I said I wanted to join the army and see the Empire, she said at once that she would use her husband's connections to get me a place. She said the money would be there to buy me a commission. But she was pleased when I told her I did not want to buy my way to promotion. She told me then that the Indian Army was the

Queen's best army because a poor man could join it and rise by merit and she will ensure I have the highest recommendations."

"That's cool," Rosie said. She told him of Cook's promise to ask Mr Harvey to teach both him and Jane to read and write. Joseph was overawed.

"You have great courage for a girl, Rosie. Cook gets very grumpy."

"Cook is nice," she said, deciding to ignore the insult to girls. By 1997 she reckoned boys and men would have learned a little bit more about girls. Why they could be so stupid about them before she had no idea.

"What's to happen to Cyril?" she said, "he deserves to go to prison."

"Lady de Courcy said I could press charges against him and Miss Payne for conspiracy. But I won't. She has been very kind to me, Rosie, and it would kill her if Master Cyril were to end up in prison."

"But the inspector took him away."

"Only for questioning, only to give him a fright. He said as much to Lady de Courcy."

"So he's going to get off scot free?"

"Lady de Courcy intends to send him out to her brother in Barbados for a year, to help on his sugar plantation. It will be hard work and a kind of punishment."

A year in Barbados seemed like heaven to Rosie, all that sunshine and swimming and wind-surfing, but she said nothing, arranging instead to meet Joseph on the roadway at half past ten. "Isn't that a little early?" he said, "Your transport doesn't leave for another half hour."

"It's in case we're unsuccessful. We might have to try a few times. If I'm too early I can walk to the village." The last thing she wanted was to be found by Mr Murray hanging around outside the hostel. The special school bus wouldn't arrive for the class till after lunch.

She left Joseph and went to the schoolroom where she

found Florence listlessly fiddling with pen and ink. She looked sad, Rosie thought.

"Hi, Florence, you wanted to see me?" she said.

The girl looked at her, "Miss Payne is right, you know. You are strange! Well, at least different," she amended, seeing Rosie's indignant expression. "Most servants call me 'Miss Florence' and wait for me to speak first. Not that I mind you not bothering with Miss. It makes you more friendly."

Rosie said nothing. There was no way she could call someone near her own age "Miss Florence".

"I want to thank you for speaking up for Joseph yesterday. Without you Mother might not have searched her room." She sighed and fiddled with the pages in front of her. A silence grew between them and Rosie began to wonder why the girl wanted to see her.

At last Florence spoke. "I shall miss my governess, Miss Payne," she said.

Rosie was astounded and was about to say something about the disgusting woman when Florence rushed on, "I know she was horrible to Joseph. But before he and Jane came here, she was so good to me. I had no friends my own age, Rosie, and she set about getting me books about children. *Jane Eyre* and *David Copperfield* and *Oliver Twist*. She talked to me about her own childhood. She was lonely too, Rosie, only much poorer than me. When Joseph and Jane came and mother approved of them, I forgot about Miss Payne for a while."

Rosie could hold her tongue no longer, "Miss Payne is bad," she said. "She was trying to ruin Joseph's life – and Jane's. They would've been split up forever and Jane would've been homeless, living rough on the streets of Dublin." She swallowed, trying to calm herself.

Florence said, "Don't you think your imagination is running away with you? You can't know any of this." When Rosie said nothing she continued, "I am sorry for Miss Payne because she has nothing to look forward to. No one else will employ her and she has no relatives. What is she to do?"

Rosie shrugged. Miss Payne was not her problem, not when she remembered Gran's story about Jane's dreadful life in the city.

"It is all Cyril's fault. He can't abide the servants unless they have no minds of their own. He put Miss Payne up to it, with the promise of friendship for life. She thought she had lost my affection and, as she often told me in the past, a woman like her depends so much on the good will of her employers. Otherwise when she is no longer useful, she is simply let go. Miss Payne has nothing, Rosie. No home, no reference."

"Has she gone yet?" Rosie asked.

"She is to leave this morning."

"Then you can give her something, can't you? Some money. Or talk to your mother. By now she might not be so angry and might write a reference for her, saying how good she was to you. She doesn't have to say anything that isn't true. That might help the woman."

Rosie did not really care what happened to Miss Payne, but she wanted to stop talking about her. She wanted to stop talking, period, and go home.

Florence's eyes lit up. "What a good idea! I knew you would think of something. I will give her money and I will persuade Mother to give her a reference. Thank you so much Rosie, you've been so helpful."

Rosie raced up to her own room, got her rucksack and changed into her jeans and sweatshirt. She would not go home in a 19th century maid's uniform from a hostelling trip. She hoped time would not play tricks on her and change her clothes back again. Sneaking down the servants' staircase, she met no one. Beneath one of the oak trees she turned to take a last look at the house. In the late October sunlight the stone was warm and mellow and the windows winked at her. The gracious drive swept up to the magnificent columns. It was beautiful.

On the first floor, she saw Lady de Courcy at the window,

her head bowed, lost in thought. Finding the necklace had not made her happy, Rosie thought, but there was nothing she could do about that. She had set out to change things for Joseph and Jane. Now there wasn't anything more she could do.

Walking along the green verge she concentrated on the future. "1997" she whispered and the trees whispered back, "1997." She set her feet marching to the rhythm and keeping her eyes on the huge iron gate she thought of nothing else.

Joseph was waiting for her.

Chapter 17

"IT'S NOT working, Joseph. I can't do it."

For ten minutes she had stood there, concentrating on home, on 1997, eyes closed, fists clenched. Nothing had happened. Joseph stood next to her, willing her departure with all his might. Now she despaired. If she were trapped here she would never see her friends again. Condemned to a life of drudgery, where people thought and dressed so differently, they might as well be from outer space.

If she stayed here, her future would be a dull routine of housework. That's if she weren't thrown out when everyone realised she wasn't a Brannigan. None of her dreams would come true. Here, she would never go to college, never become an engineer, never travel abroad. Instead she'd have to learn to keep her mouth shut and not offer any opinions to someone like Mr Harvey. So many people would think they were her betters. She would spend her whole life being told what to do by others; it was unbearable.

Pacing up and down, she was on the verge of tears. How could she get home?

It was Joseph who found an answer. "When we came back here, you were holding the necklace. It gave us extra power as if it were drawing us back. If you have something strong that belongs to your time maybe that will help."

Rosie thought. Obviously clothes were no use, or the rucksack. But . . . what about the tape? Nothing was more state-of-the-art late twentieth century than that.

She took it from the bag, pressed playback until it clicked back at the start. Then she turned to Joseph, "Don't pass out when you hear this. It's a machine that records voices."

He was mystified and she tried to be clearer. "Like, if you say something and I press a button, the machine hears what you say and can repeat it afterwards, in your voice."

The boy paled, "That's not natural," he said, "a machine speaking."

"It's what happened yesterday," Rosie said, "when you heard Cyril and Miss Payne in the great hall. Now I hope you'll hear Mr Murray, my teacher."

Joseph would have liked to ask a hundred questions but time was running out. Glancing up the avenue he saw a procession of people moving towards the side of the house. The tenants were on their way to pay their respects. Soon questions would be raised about Rosie. Mrs Brannigan was not too clever, but she could get mightily upset if she thought someone had taken her daughter's position in the great house. Rosie could stay no longer. He gripped her arm and she pressed "play."

"1997 and Home," she prayed while Joseph whispered, "Good-bye Rosie."

"Towards the end of the last century, in this house, a young boy was employed to do odd jobs and work in the garden. He arrived out of nowhere, ragged and dirty, with his younger sister in tow."

Startled, Joseph stepped away. The tape crackled then whizzed forward and the last words he heard were, *"Some time I shall be back."* They were repeated over and over. The volume got louder till the words filled Joseph's head. Hands over his ears, he turned and ran.

Halfway up the drive he halted and looked back.

Rosie was gone.

Weak with relief, Rosie sat on the verge and absorbed the sounds of a distant car, a tractor in a nearby field. A plane flew overhead and she would have danced for joy if she'd any strength. She was facing the long drive and she could see figures moving at the side of the house.

Her heart sank. For a second she thought they were the tenants of a few minutes ago and that time had lost its grip, mixing the two centuries. Then as the group emerged from the shadows, she saw their clothes, heard their distant voices. Her classmates. They would not be leaving till after lunch, when the school minibus would arrive to take them home. For a few moments Rosie looked at them fondly, wondering if David Byrne had managed to stay out of trouble. Probably not. She was looking forward to the stories he would tell her next week. Some day she might recount her own adventures, when they knew each other better, and he was less likely to think she was mad.

Rosie got up and walked towards the village. She had gone a short distance when the bus caught up with her and she hailed it. When the doors swished back she found herself facing a familiar face and groaned. He would throw her off the bus.

Instead his eyes shifted from hers and he said, "Fare please."

As she walked down the aisle, the driver sniffed. He was sure she was the same kid who'd cheeked him before. A right eejit he'd made of himself on her account, calling in to that hostel yesterday and insisting on seeing Mr Harvey, the teacher in charge.

Instead he'd met a Mr Murray, a young whipper-snapper, who'd told him none of his lot had been let loose the day before. And when the driver had described them, Mr Murray had looked at him with concern, asked him about his health, hinted perhaps he shouldn't be driving, especially not a bus full of passengers.

"You know," the young teacher had leaned over and patted his arm, "It's a medical fact that people can be in the same job too long. It causes stress, d'you see! And that has peculiar effects."

Cheek! No wonder the kids in his charge were the way they were. Still, he wasn't going to take this one on again.

"We weren't expecting you till this evening," Mom said when she arrived at lunch time.

"The bus was early," Rosie said, more or less truthfully.

"You won't believe what happened during the week." Gran was dying to tell her the news and Rosie composed her expression, while the old lady said dramatically, "It's lucky your mother gave Mr Brennan a spare key, because on Thursday night, when we were all out, Mr Brennan heard noises."

She looked at her granddaughter who widened her eyes in an attempt to appear impressed.

"When he came in he found a big young fellow, a couple of years older than you. Very tough looking, Mr Brennan said." Rosie almost smiled. The description did not fit Joseph. "There was a terrible struggle. Mr Brennan could have been injured by a big fellow like that. But he's a brave man with no regard for his own safety. He almost had the lad, but he slipped out of his jacket and got away."

"Did he take anything, Gran?"

"Oddly enough, not much. Just a couple of old coats."

"That's terrible." Try as she might, Rosie could not get shock and horror into her voice, but Gran didn't notice.

"A couple of old coats! He took my lovely green lurex jacket," Mom said, "and that biker's jacket your father was so fond of. Not that that's any loss. But my lurex was a designer label." This time Rosie gasped. She had forgotten the jackets. She wondered if Mrs Smiley had found the lurex and what she thought of it.

Gran sniffed, "That green thing looked like a set of traffic lights. It must've been designed by a road engineer. But your father used to cut a fine figure in the leather jacket, Rosie. I remember him wearing it when he'd call for your mother before they were married."

"A pity he never had the Harley-Davidson to go with it," Mom said, "It didn't look right with the old Vespa." Then she said sarcastically, "Anyway, if your father wants an old jacket, can't he take the one that thug left behind. That's *very* old."

"I must show it to you Rosie," Gran got up at once and went off, returning in a few moments with Joseph's tweed jacket. Rosie had never noticed that the elbows sagged or how frayed the collar was. She fingered the material with affection.

"Guess what we found inside one of the pockets," Gran said, "two gold sovereigns with Queen Victoria's head on them and dated 1870 and a fancy wooden whistle with the initials 'JON' carved on it. The police took them away, said they were probably from another robbery. They just left us with this." She shook the jacket.

Rosie could not resist it. "1870. JON," she said, "Didn't you say Joseph O'Neill worked in Oak Park in 1870, Gran? And that he could travel through time. Maybe he came back to search for the necklace you told me about, the one you said was missing."

"Don't be ridiculous," Gran said, as Rosie had known she would. "You know I never believed any of that time travel nonsense."

Mom sighed, "A pity you ever told it to Rosie then. She has such a vivid imagination."

Mischievously and with a straight face her daughter said, "Gran said time travelling is a gift that skips the generations in our family. I wonder if I've got it?"

"Don't be daft!" They spoke in unison this time.

Rosie grinned to herself.

"Whoever the intruder was, he was certainly very strange," Mom mused. "He left the telly on, so he must have watched it and and he put on the washing machine and tried to cook an egg in the microwave. It exploded and left a terrible mess. The police said it's not usual for a robber to watch telly and cook on the premises he's robbing. Very odd . . ."

It was two months later and one day, after school, Rosie was fixing a sandwich for herself in the kitchen. Her parents were at work and Gran was watching Sky News. Suddenly there was an excited yell from the sitting-room.

"Rosie . . . quick! Come in and watch this." She rushed in. Gran was pointing at the screen. There, laid out in a glass case, was the Oak Park diamond necklace.

"What . . . ?" Rosie gasped.

"Listen, listen." Gran hushed her.

The newscaster gave the details. "Today saw a record price for the de Courcy necklace at Christy's auction house in London. This necklace has as its centre piece a unique diamond, and was presented to Lord de Courcy by the Maharajah of Kashmir in the early 1850s. His lordship, who resided at Oak Park, County Wicklow, later gave the jewels to his wife as an anniversary gift. The gems have been missing for more than a century, but recently came to light when Felicity Brooks, the great-great-granddaughter of Lady de Courcy, made the discovery in a trunk belonging to her ancestor. Miss Brooks told Sky News that Lady de Courcy believed the necklace had brought only trouble to her family and had therefore hidden it away. Today the de Beers diamond company paid a record two million pounds for the item."

Gran and Rosie looked at each other. Gran shook her head. "That blessed necklace brought so much trouble for poor Lady de Courcy. It made her realise what a vicious man her son was. I'm not surprised she hid it away. But I'm glad the mystery of its whereabouts is solved at last."

It was later that week that Gran came home from the Gilbert Library and showed Rosie a photograph and a short paragraph from an old newspaper.

"I went through all the copies of *The Irish Times* from 1870, wishing to find some mention of Joseph," she said. "Of course there was very little hope and I might have given up except that other items of news kept my interest. But today I opened the edition for March 15, 1890 and this is what I saw." She gave Rosie the photocopy, which she read avidly:

Captain Joseph O'Neill, of her Majesty's Indian Army and veteran hero of the 3rd Anglo-Burmese War, is on leave in Dublin, convalescing from war wounds. After an absence of many years Capt O'Neill has been reunited with his sister Jane, now Mrs Rafferty.

One of the few Irishmen to enlist in her Majesty's forces as a private and rise through the ranks, Capt O'Neill is considered by his superiors to possess the qualities of bravery and intelligence in equal measure. His reunion with his sister was joyful, their first meeting for many years.

Captain O'Neill's wife and children remain in Burma. He will rejoin his regiment and family in three months time.

"Isn't it marvellous, Rosie? They did keep in touch. All those stories were wrong. And Joseph did so well."

"He got his wish," Rosie murmured. He had fulfilled his ambition and had not lost contact with Jane. Mr Harvey must have taught them to read and write. She thought of the butler and Mrs Biddle and hoped they'd been happy. Mrs Smiley too.

Her journey to 1870 had been a dreadful strain on her powers. For a while it had been very doubtful that she would get back. She had felt so afraid. Could she ever face such fear again? Was it worth the outcome?

"I'm so pleased at the way things turned out," Gran told her. "The necklace turned up and it's obvious Joseph didn't lose his good name. And the great thing is that he and Jane never lost contact with each other. That's given me such peace of mind."

Rosie smiled. Gran was right. Things had turned out well. All the risks had been worthwhile.

The End